Mahalia

A Gospel Musical

by Tom Stolz

A SAMUEL FRENCH ACTING EDITION

SAMUEL FRENCH

FOUNDED 1830

NEW YORK HOLLYWOOD LONDON TORONTO

SAMUELFRENCH.COM

RENTAL AND MUSIC MATERIALS

An orchestration, consisting of **Conductor's Score, Organ Score, Piano Score, and Vocal Scores,** will be loaned two months prior to the production ONLY on the receipt of the Licensing Fee quoted for all performances, the rental fee and a refundable deposit.

Please contact Samuel French for perusal of the music materials as well as a performance license application.

The Original Cast Recording of *MAHALIA*, is available from Samuel French, Inc., at samuelfrench.com. A recording of the sound effects used in *MAHALIA*, is available from: Promised Land Productions, Inc. / 5090 Covington St. / Excelsior, MN 55331

**IMPORTANT BILLING AND CREDIT
REQUIREMENTS**

All producers of *MAHALIA must* give credit to the Author of the Play in all programs distributed in connection with performances of the Play, and in all instances in which the title of the Play appears for the purposes of advertising, publicizing or otherwise exploiting the Play and/ or a production. The name of the Author *must* appear on a separate line on which no other name appears, immediately following the title and *must* appear in size of type not less than fifty percent of the size of the title type.

MAHALIA was first produced at the Old Log Theater in Excelsior, Minnesota on January 27, 1994. The performance was directed by Don Stolz, with sets and lighting by Jon Stolz, and costumes by Wayne Murphey. The production stage manager was Monty Hicks. The cast was as follows:

Jearlyn Steele Battle as Mahalia

Fred Steele

Gloria Taylor-James

AUTHOR'S NOTES

This play is written for three actors. One actor plays Mahalia throughout. Another actor plays all the remaining female roles and must play piano, while the remaining actor plays all the male roles and must play piano and organ. All music and singing is performed live by the three actors.

The staging should be minimal consisting of risers and platform upstage that represent the steps to the Lincoln Memorial, as well as other locales. These risers may also be used for the "Heavenly Choir" if a choir is incorporated into the finale. There should also be steps from the stage into the audience.

MAHALIA depends more on lighting, with colored cyclorama and other effects, to create scenes, change mood, or make transitions. And, of course, the music.

There is a grand piano stage right and a Hammond B3 organ with Leslie speaker stage left. Both keyboards should face offstage. A small table with telephone is located near the organ. A small lectern that can be easily moved is used as a church pulpit and speaking rostrum. Three bentwood chairs representing living rooms, automobiles, church pews, etc., are used throughout the play and are moved in and out of position by the actors. There is a bench down left, which is used for the train and also for the limousine. There is also a bentwood chair down right. A few costume changes are used to show character or time change. There are also a few hand props.

-Tom Stolz

THE MUSIC FOR MAHALIA

ACT I

Careless Love Blues .... W.C. Handy

© 1926, 1953. Columbia Records recording by Bessie Smith with Louis Armstrong on cornet used with permission by Handy Bros. Music, Inc. and Columbia Records

Hand Me Down Yo' Silver Trumpet, Gabriel .... Negro Spiritual

Let Us Go Down To Jordan........................Negro Spiritual

Jim Crow Blues............................... F. Steele/T. Stolz

© 1993. Used with permission by Promised Land Prod., Inc.

Yes, God Is Real ....Kenneth Morris

© 1972. Used with permission by Morris Music Co., Inc. BMI

Joshua Fit The Battle Of Jericho .... Negro Spiritual

Didn't It Rain................................... Negro Spiritual

I'm Going To Live The Life I Sing About In My Songs ......T.A. Dorsey

© 1941. Used with permission by Unichappell Music Inc. BMI

City Called Heaven .... Negro Spiritual

How I Got Over .... W.H. Brewster

ACT II

We Shall Overcome .... Adapted from "I'll Overcome Some Day" by Charles Tindley

Keep Your Hand On The Plow..................... Negro Spiritual

I've Been Buked............................... Negro Spiritual

Deep River .... Negro Spiritual

Dig A Little Deeper .... Kenneth Morris

© 1975. Used with permission by Morris Music Co., Inc. BMI

Walk in Jerusalem .... Negro Spiritual

Elijah Rock.....................................Negro Spiritual

I'm On My Way .... Negro Spiritual

Take My Hand, Precious Lord ....T. A. Dorsey

© 1938. Used with permission by Unichappell Music Inc. BMI

Move On Up A Little Higher .......................W.H. Brewster

© 1946. Used with permission by Unichappell Music Inc. BMI

Behold,
the Lord thy God hath set the Promised Land before thee:
go up and possess it,
as the Lord God of thy fathers hath said unto thee;
fear not, neither be discouraged.

Deuteronomy 1.21

ACT I

*(As the house lights go down, we hear the Columbia recording of Bessie Smith singing **Careless Love**:)*

LOVE, OH LOVE, OH CARELESS LOVE,
YOU FLY TO MY HEAD LIKE WINE
YOU'VE WRECKED THE LIFE OF A MANY POOR GAL
AND YOU NEARLY SPOILED THIS LIFE OF MINE.

*(The curtain rises and the lights come up to reveal **FRED** and his cousin **MAHALIA** as she sings to the recording. Her imitation of Bessie Smith is perfect.)*

MAHALIA. *(singing)*
LOVE, OH LOVE, OH CARELESS LOVE,

COUSIN FRED. Let it out, Mahalia, you got it! Let it out!

MAHALIA. *(singing)*
IN YOUR CLUTCHES OF DESIRE

COUSIN FRED. Girl, you sound more like Bessie Smith than Bessie Smith!

MAHALIA. *(singing)*
YOU'VE MADE ME BREAK A MANY TRUE VOW
THEN YOU SET MY VERY SOUL ON FIRE...

AUNT DUKE. *(enters from right wearing hat, coat, gloves, and carrying purse)* Ragtime jazz, indecent! Blues! Turn that devil music off!

*(**MAHALIA** stops singing and **FRED** turns victrola off.)*

Bessie Smith with her Careless Love! I won't have that mess in my house!

COUSIN FRED. Oh, Mama, we just having a little fun. Nothing wrong with that. This house could stand a little fun.

AUNT DUKE. You be quiet! This is my business. When her mother died I promised to make that child do! Halie, you stay in the path. Church got plenty music, you mind me? You going learn to do right and you going learn to work! *(with derision as she removes her hat and coat)* Careless love!

(Exits left.)

COUSIN FRED. Don't you worry. Someday the sun going shine down on you, way up north in St. Louis or Chicago.

MAHALIA. You think so cousin Fred?

COUSIN FRED. Baby, I seen it. You going be famous in this world. You going walk with kings and queens.

AUNT DUKE. *(entering, putting apron on)* Well, right now she walking with the devil! *(to **MAHALIA**)* You better put yourself on the sinner's bench at church and ask God's forgiveness! *(to **FRED**)* And you! You come in and help me. And stop filling that girl's mind with worldly things!

(They exit left.)

MAHALIA. *(to audience)* My Aunt Duke going make sure the devil don't get no help from this house. And in Pinching Town, New Orleans, 1927, the devil be doing some of his best work! *(The lights change as she moves downstage.)* New Orleans was a singing, dancing city. Music on the Mississippi showboats, brass bands, Mardi Gras. Storeyville, with its honky-tonks and "sportin' houses." Jelly Roll Morton, King Oliver, ragtime, jazz, blues, all pouring in through every window. Ma Rainey, the "Mama of Blues." And Bessie Smith! People lined up for blocks buying her records. Might not have coal, but got more fire out of her. Ooo, those songs risky; risky with the devil! And it didn't help none he'd stole God's holy beat. But my Aunt Duke got me fixed firmly in the pew at Mt. Moriah Baptist Church.

AUNT DUKE. *(enters from left)* No cards, no high life, and no lowdown jazz!

(She exits.)

MAHALIA. *(to audience)* Saturday's payday and people are "good-timing." New Orleans is jumpin' with music. But after Saturday comes Sunday's song, and they's joy in those sanctified churches. Joy in the Holy Ghost and joy in the brilliance of God's glory. Everybody singing and clapping their hands, stomping their feet, praising God with their whole bodies! We had a beat, a powerful beat, a rhythm we held on to from slavery days. Jubilees were quick to bring the shout, send those "sanctified saints" dancing in high spirits. Dancing was a holy thing if you were dancing in the spirit. Outside you were stepping with the devil. Sing to the Lord! Shout to His glory! Dance to His Holy name!

(AUNT DUKE and PASTOR LAWRENCE enter from right. They all sing Hand Me Down Yo' Silver Trumpet, Gabriel.)

ALL.
O HAN ME DOWN (HAN ME DOWN)
HAN ME DOWN (HAN ME DOWN)
HAN ME DOWN YO' SILVER TRUMPET, GABRIEL
HAN ME DOWN (HAN ME DOWN)
HAN ME DOWN (HAN ME DOWN
HAN ME DOWN YO' SILVER TRUMPET LORD, OH LORD.

AUNT DUKE. *(singing to PASTOR LAWRENCE, referring to MAHALIA)*
YOU SEE THAT GIRL SHE DRESSED SO FINE?

MAHALIA. *(singing)*
HAN ME DOWN YO' SILVER TRUMPET, GABRIEL.

AUNT DUKE. *(singing)*
WELL, SHE AIN'T GOT JESUS ON HER MIND.

ALL. *(singing)*
HAN ME DOWN YO' SILVER TRUMPET, LORD.
(Repeat chorus.)

THE REV. LAWRENCE. She's ready for the water, but she can't be baptized without your "yes." Don't stand in her way; she's old enough to know.

AUNT DUKE. Pastor Lawrence, she ain't going to go in that Mississippi River no dry devil and come out a wet one! When she come out she going have something that carry her everywhere she go. She going have Jesus!

MAHALIA. But Aunt Duke, I found Jesus! I had a vision. I wasn't asleep and I wasn't awake. I was…in the spirit.

AUNT DUKE. Humph.

MAHALIA. I was traveling in green pastures and I came upon my mama. I am seeking for the Lord, Mama. She said, "Search among the flowers, you'll find Him there." But how will I know Him from any other man? She said, "You will know Him, because He wears salvation on His brow." So I turned around…and I saw Him. *(singing)* Jesus my God, I know your name. Then He put out His hand and touched me.

AUNT DUKE. *(amazed)* She has been reborn.

THE REV. LAWRENCE. The spirit of God is too high to explain! Let us go down to the Jordan!

(**AUNT DUKE** *agrees and they all sing* **Let Us Go Down To Jordan** *as they put a white baptismal gown on* **MAHALIA** *and walk downstage to the Mississippi.*)

AUNT DUKE.
LET US GO DOWN TO
ALL.
JORDAN
AUNT DUKE.
LET US GO DOWN TO
ALL.
JORDAN
AUNT DUKE.
LET US GO DOWN TO
ALL.
JORDAN
RELIGION IS SO SWEET
AUNT DUKE.
YOU MUST BELIEVE TO BE BAPTIZED

ALL.

BE BAPTIZED

ALL.

BE BAPTIZED

AUNT DUKE.

YOU MUST BELIEVE TO BE BAPTIZED

ALL.

RELIGION IS SO SWEET

MAHALIA.

I'M GOIN' DOWN TO JORDAN TO

ALL.

GIT BAPTIZED

ALL.

GIT BAPTIZED

ALL.

GIT BAPTIZED

MAHALIA.

I'M GOIN' DOWN TO JORDAN TO GIT BAPTIZED

ALL.

RELIGION IS SO SWEET

THE REV. LAWRENCE. *(They wade in the water.)* I baptize you, Mahalia Jackson, according to the faith. *(***LAWRENCE** *dunks* **MAHALIA** *below the surface.)* In the name of the Father and of the Son and of the Holy Ghost.

AUNT DUKE & THE REV. LAWRENCE. Amen!

*(***MAHALIA** *is out of breath now as* **LAWRENCE** *has taken his own sweet time. Her eyes are getting bigger but she is returned to the surface, reborn a new creature, her hands clapping with joy.)*

AUNT DUKE. *(to* **PASTOR***)* She has a new look.

THE REV. LAWRENCE. She got the Holy Ghost now!

(They remove the baptismal gown and exit left as Center lights fade. **MAHALIA** *moves downstage Right.)*

MAHALIA. *(looking up to God)* Lord, I hope You been taking notice of me lately 'cause You got to help Halie. I want to make something with myself. I want to go to school in Chicago and be a nurse. But how can I do that with Aunt Duke always holding me down? Lord, I know You brought your children out of Egypt, but You really got Your work cut out for You with Aunt Duke!

(Lights come up on center acting area. **AUNT DUKE** *enters from left.)*

AUNT DUKE. You leave Halie be! Up there with all those Chicago gangsters. You trying to ruin that girl?

COUSIN FRED. *(following)* I'm trying to help her, Mama, so she can have a chance in life! Maybe even have a little fun.

AUNT DUKE. This is her fun right here; looking at me. I'm the fun!

COUSIN FRED. You want her spending the rest of her life like you? Slaving away for Mr. and Mrs. Plant. Dressing their children, cooking their food, washing their dirty clothes.

AUNT DUKE. Go along with your gamblin' men and your music men!

COUSIN FRED. You want her ironing old man Plant's shirts 'til she's too old and tired to get up and leave this Jim Crow town?

AUNT DUKE. Go on! Get to your sportin' life!

COUSIN FRED. Negroes got it better up North. She can ride in streetcars and sit where she wants. She can go in a restaurant and eat. She can try on a dress in a white man's store before she buys it! Don't you know? She wants to be a nurse, heal people. That's how she wants to serve her Jesus. What chance she got here where a million dollars won't buy her an unsegregated glass of water? Jim Crow got her chained up like some Mississippi mule.

AUNT DUKE. *(crosses left picks up Bible then crosses right to* **MAHALIA***)* Seek the Lord where He may be found. Serve Him in the days of thy youth. *(hands her the Bible)* You find yourself a good Baptist Church. It's cold in Chicago.

MAHALIA. Don't you worry. Won't nothing get between Halie and her God! I'm a Baptist bred, and a Baptist born, and when I die, I'll be a Baptist gone!

(**AUNT DUKE** *takes money from the front of her dress and gives it to* **MAHALIA** *who transfers it down the front of her dress. She kisses* **AUNT DUKE** *goodbye and crosses Left to give* **FRED** *a hug. She takes suitcase and sweater he has ready for her and takes a step or two left. She stops and looks up to where God is watching.*)

That was fast work, Lord.

(*She crosses left and takes her seat on the Illinois Central. We hear the sound of a train whistle as the lights fade on all but* **MAHALIA** *and a man singing the blues.*)

BLUES MAN.
I'M TIRED OF N' ORLEANS,
GONNA LEAVE THIS JIM CROW TOWN
YES, I'M TIRED OF N' ORLEANS
JIM CROW ALWAYS PUT ME DOWN
I'LL BE LEAVIN' HERE TOMORROW
I'M SWEET CHICAGO BOUND
YES, I'M GOIN' UP NORTH
THEY SAY THE MONEY GROWS ON TREES
NO, I DON'T GIVE A DOGGONE
IF MY BLACK SOUL LEAVES
THEY SAY IT'S COLD IN CHICAGO
GONNA PACK MY BVDs

(*The lights fade on the* **BLUES MAN** *as we hear the train pulling out of the station.* **MAHALIA** *reads Psalm 40 from her Bible.*)

I waited patiently for the Lord; and He inclined unto me, and heard my cry. He brought me up also out of an horrible pit, out of the miry clay, and set my feet upon a rock, and established my goings. And He hath put a new song in my mouth, (*music intro*) even praise unto our God: many shall hear it and shall trust in the Lord.

*(With Bible in her lap, she sings **Yes, God is Real**.)*

MAHALIA. *(cont.)* THERE ARE SOME THINGS I MAY NOT KNOW
THERE ARE SOME PLACES, OH LORD, I CAN NOT GO
BUT I AM SURE OF THIS ONE THING
THAT GOD IS REAL, FOR I CAN FEEL HIM IN MY SOUL

YES, GOD IS REAL, OH HE'S REAL IN MY SOUL
YES, GOD IS REAL, FOR HE HAS WASHED AND MADE ME
   WHOLE
OOH, HIS LOVE FOR ME IS LIKE PURE GOLD, OH YES IT IS
YES, GOD IS REAL, FOR I CAN FEEL HIM IN MY SOUL

(We hear the sound of the train whistle fading in the distance as the lights fade.)

(to audience as lights come up on center area) Oh, it wasn't the "Promised Land." But when I stepped off that train, the south side of Chicago was a miracle to me. It was a Negro city. Negro policemen, Negro firemen and schoolteachers, Negro doctors and lawyers and aldermen. Never before had Negroes lived so well and had so much money. Driving up and down Michigan Boulevard in their big shiny touring cars. Men strolling in the evening wearing derbies and spats, carrying walking sticks. Their women with diamonds and fur coats, leading little dogs on leashes. Millionaires living in mansions. Oh yes, in Chicago our people were advancing! And all the jazz musicians come up from New Orleans and Memphis and St. Louis. White folks were coming out in crowds to the Grand Terrace Ballroom to hear Louis Armstrong and Earl "Father" Hines play their "Loosiana jazz." And Bessie Smith was singing at the Vendome! But I kept my promise to Aunt Duke and The Greater Salem Baptist Church became my home. I was singing in the choir and with The Johnson Gospel Singers. Five of us; the first gospel group in Chicago. We were singing in small storefront churches all over the south side. But tonight, we were singing in our first big church! *(piano intro, as **MAHALIA** looks up.)* Lord, You sure puttin' Halie up! Hallelujah!

*(She sings **Joshua Fit The Battle Of Jericho**.)*

JOSHUA FIT THE BATTLE OF JERICHO, JERICHO, JERICHO,
JOSHUA FIT THE BATTLE OF JERICHO
AND THE WALLS CAME TUMBLIN' DOWN
JOSHUA FIT THE BATTLE OF JERICHO, JERICHO, JERICHO,
JOSHUA FIT THE BATTLE OF JERICHO
AND THE WALLS CAME TUMBLIN' DOWN.

*(During the piano solo, **MAHALIA** "lets loose" with her "holy dance," emphasizing certain textural points with her body. All is brought to a halt by the **PASTOR**'s wrath.)*

PASTOR. *(enter left)* Blasphemous! Get that twisting and that jazz out of this church!

MAHALIA. *(to audience)* Uh, oh!

PASTOR. Shame! Shame! It's a disgrace! In God's own house!

MAHALIA. *(to **PASTOR**)* This the way we sing down South. I been singing this way in church all my life.

PASTOR. This…this…shouting and bouncing and clapping. It's an offense against God!

MAHALIA. Hold a minute, baby! I am serving God! You read the Bible and you'll see. Right there in Psalm 47, "Oh clap your hands, all ye people; shout unto the Lord with the voice of triumph." I'm doing what the Bible tells me to do! I got no right not to sing! It's a gift of the Lord for His glory!

*(The **PASTOR** storms off and **MAHALIA** comes downstage center to audience.)*

The Bible say the common people heard Jesus gladly, and it's true. Most people thought gospel singing was like a letter from down home. But those big "society" churches looked down their noses at me. But when the Great Depression hit, it was like someone pulled the switch. The South Side just stopped running. The diamonds and the furs disappeared and people weren't pulling up to those big churches in their fine cars any more. The collection box was empty and things got desperate. *(piano vamp)* That's when the doors were opened wide to Mahalia Jackson and The Johnson Gospel Singers; 'cause when we sang, people came. And the walls came tumblin' down! *(looking up)* God, You sure know Your business! *(singing)*

MAHALIA. *(cont.)* UP TO DE WALLS OB JERICHO
HE MARCHED WITH SWORD DRAWN IN HIS HAN';
"GO BLOW DEM RAM HORNS," CRIED JOSHUA,
"KASE DE BATTLE AM IN MY HAN'." JOSHUA FIT THE BATTLE
   OF JERICHO, JERICHO, JERICHO,
JOSHUA FIT THE BATTLE OF JERICHO
AND THE WALLS CAME TUMBLIN' DOWN.

*(After song, **DORSEY** enters from left and crosses to her.)*

DORSEY. *(applauding her performance)* Miss Jackson, when you sing you add more flowers and feathers than anybody, and they're all exactly right.

MAHALIA. That's not me, that's God. He gives it to me. I'm just the instrument.

DORSEY. Amen, sister, amen! My name's Dorsey, Thomas Dors…

MAHALIA. Honey, you think I don't know you? *(to audience as **DORSEY** arranges two chairs at center)* They used to call him "Georgia Tom," songwriter and blues player for Ma Rainey's Rabbit Foot Minstrels; until the Lord needed some gospel and snatched him away. *(to **DORSEY** as they sit)* You been doing some mighty fine "Kingdom work" with your gospel songs. But gospel singing something new to some of these preachers up North. They say you can't sing the gospel, you can only preach the gospel. *(said just loud enough for the **PASTOR** to hear)*

DORSEY. I believe they're jealous. You accomplish in one song what they can't accomplish in a two-hour sermon. *(He is carried off by his own thoughts.)* Gospel singing broadcasts the "good news" and nothing prepares the heart for the reception of God's "Word" as do gospel songs, sung with spirit and faith. They bring good tidings about salvation as they find their place in the hearts of God's children, edifying the believer and glorifying God.

MAHALIA. *(There is a slight pause as* **MAHALIA** *takes all this in.)* Uh huh.

DORSEY. And no one can hurt the gospel because the gospel is strong, like a two-edged sword. Strong enough to cut through to the soul, no matter if Satan himself sings a gospel song.

MAHALIA. He better not be playing your piano.

DORSEY. Well, some people say I'm still writing the blues, but I'm not. I'm writing gospel. The gospel of people standing with God in an open field. The blues is a person standing alone in a deep pit, crying for help. Gospel songs are songs of hope. And they come into being by divine design, not like ordinary songs. That's why I believe it's a little bit off to use the power of music just for entertainment. It seems that power ought to be reserved for the Word of God.

MAHALIA. *(pause)* You rest now, honey.

DORSEY. Miss Jackson, you have a sense of oneness with your respondents…a wonderful ability to capture the communal spirit of a performance.

MAHALIA. Say what?

DORSEY. And the combination of your natural appeal and blues presence, along with your spirituality, would convey the sentiment of my new more emotive gospels.

MAHALIA. You don't say?.

DORSEY. That's why I would like you to go on the road with me.

MAHALIA. *(suspicious)* On the road, darlin'?

DORSEY. To bring my songs to life. We'll play the gospel circuit. Churches, revivals, gospel tents, the National Baptist Convention. We'll bring in some souls and ease our own.

MAHALIA. *(pause)* That be good.

DORSEY. And, of course, with you demonstrating my songs, we'll sell a lot of sheet music. Ten cents apiece. That's where the real money is.

MAHALIA. Ten cents?

DORSEY. It adds up.

MAHALIA. You the Lord's first traveling salesman.

DORSEY. I hope you won't say "no."

MAHALIA. I never say "no" 'til I know what I'm "no-ing." Be right back. *(rises and crosses downstage right)* God, what You want? I come up to Chicago to be a nurse but maybe You got some other kind of healing in mind. Halie can't think like You do, Lord, so if You want me going on the road with this man over here, You going have to tell me. *(She waits a moment for the answer, then returns to* **DORSEY**.*)* The Lord say He want me to go.

DORSEY. *(rises)* Yes, I know. I've already spoken with Him. *(exit Right)*

MAHALIA. *(to God and all)* Lord, there ain't no turning back now! Why turn back on joy? We travelling the gospel highway, rolling on! Philadelphia, St. Louis, Detroit; bound for glory, Amen! *(to audience as lights come up center)* Oh yes, the Lord had given us our marchin' orders, "Go ye into all the world and preach the gospel to every creature." And we did. Five years of one-night stands and living out of suitcases. We were "fish and bread" singers. Singing for God, as well as for our supper.

*(***DORSEY*** enters from right and crosses to left of* **MAHALIA**. *He is counting the money.)*

What's the matter? You look like death on a soda cracker.

DORSEY. Everybody talking 'bout heaven ain't going there! Someone been fooling with the money. There's more due us.

MAHALIA. Lord, they's a lot of trickeration in the world!

DORSEY. I thought that last promoter looked a little devious. *(He hands* **MAHALIA** *her share.)*

MAHALIA. Devious? Baby, that man a snake trying to walk. Still, it pays to serve Jesus! *(MAHALIA adds money to the growing wad retrieved from her bosom.)* Where we at next?

DORSEY. Bessemer Alabama.

MAHALIA. *(with apprehension)* Alabama?

DORSEY. "The Back To God Day."

MAHALIA. You got extra gas, case the "man" don't sell us none?

DORSEY. In the trunk. Got plenty food and coffee too.

MAHALIA. *(to no one in particular)* Got the money but he won't sell. Won't let us use the washroom either. *(looking up)* That's the worst part, Lord. Can't even relieve yourself like decent folk.

DORSEY. Lord didn't promise a smooth road, just a sure one. *(He exits right.)*

MAHALIA. That's right. And everywhere we went, gospel music was a mighty force. Breaking down the color line. Teaching people's hearts what their minds didn't know. 'cause darlin's, there's no great and no small among us. We great when we got God's love and we small only when we reject Him. And who would dare reject Him? No, you can't hate God. And babies, there's something of God in every one of us. Well, then, the depression was over. The switch was turned back on and people warn't poor as Job's turkey anymore. That's when the Lord had something new in His mind, and it warn't five and dime sheet music either.

DORSEY. *(entering from right)* Records! That's where the future is. The Good Lord is going into the recording business!

MAHALIA. *(to audience)* You can't out-think God!

DORSEY. Here, this is yours. *(hands MAHALIA some money)* Got some new songs for you to learn, get recording right away. *(starts to exit left)* Hey, let me know what you think of "Peace In The Valley." I wrote that one just for you and nobody else. Put your name on it. Mahalia Jackson, "The Queen" of gospel singers! "The Queen!" *(exit left)*

MAHALIA. If you believe in God, He will open the windows of heaven and shower blessings upon you. *(She deposits money in the usual place.)* And didn't it rain children? Didn't it rain, oh my Lord! It rained gold! I recorded a song for Apollo called "Move On Up A Little Higher," and it flashed across the sky like lightnin'. It moved on up so fast we couldn't keep track of it. Colored folks were buying it in New York, Detroit, Chicago, California. A hundred thousand copies sold overnight. Then two hundred thousand. Then a million! Apollo couldn't keep up. Finally, two million copies! "Move On Up" hit the top and became my trademark. And it made me rich too! Over three hundred thousand dollars in one year! *(looking up)* Thank you Jesus! *(to audience)* They don't make 'em like Jesus anymore! That record made me famous too. Demands for appearances started pourin' in. People wanting me to sing here or appear there. Churches, concerts, radio. Touring all over the country. *(to God)* 'Scuse me, God. I ain't complaining, you know that. But there been more piano players revolutin' 'round here than horses on a merry-go-round. Now, Halie can't fool around with all these different piano players anymore. I need somebody who can stick, and I mean stick their behind in that seat and stay. And it ain't going be easy 'cause you know, Lord, can't just anybody play for me. I need somebody who can get my style.

MILDRED. *(enters from left)* Excuse me, Miss Jackson. I'm Mildred Falls.

(**MAHALIA** *looks over at* **MILDRED**, *then up to God, then back to* **MILDRED**.)

MAHALIA. You the new piano player I just sent for?

MILDRED. Yes, Miss Jackson.

MAHALIA. Can you play?

MILDRED. Yes, Miss Jackson.

MAHALIA. Let's hear.

(**MILDRED** *sits down at the piano and starts to play. She gets about four notes out.)*

MAHALIA. *(cont.)* That's good, baby, you'll do.

MILDRED. Thank you, Miss Jackson. *(exit right)*

MAHALIA. *(looking up)* Lord, you pilin' Halie's plate higher than she can handle! And Lord, I know you won't mind; Halie going buy herself a great big brand new Buick Roadmaster. Hallelujah! *(to audience)* Oh yes, I was rich now. And famous. But only with Negroes. I still lived far inside the colored world and scarcely even knew a single white person. But the Lord was studyin' on that too.

MILDRED. *(rushes in from right)* Miracle come to pass! Halie, look at here! *(reading invitation)* Professor Stearns and The Institute Of Jazz Studies invites you to a symposium on "The Origins Of Jazz Music" to be held at Music Inn, located in Lennox, Massachusetts. *(to* **MAHALIA***)* This Professor Stearns make it sound pretty easy. Just want you to come up and show the musicologists what gospel music is all about.

MAHALIA. *(takes invitation)* What's a musicologist?

MILDRED. Don't ask me. *(takes invitation back)* Got no more idea than if it was the man in the moon.

MAHALIA. Well, baby, I got less 'cause I can see the man in the moon. *(grabs invitation)* Could have two heads and six piano legs all I know. *(studying invitation)* They going have anthropologists and sociologists too.

MILDRED. Let's see. *(takes invitation)* Lordy! Here some poor man that got himself a Guggenheim Fellowship! Mahalia, you finally made it into the white folks world and look where it landed you. *(She laughs.)*

MAHALIA. Feel like we headed for that French whatchamacallit...take your head off! *(to audience)* So, Mildred and I drove on up to this Music Inn near some lake in Massachusetts and that Professor Stearns met us and showed us where we would stay the night and all like that. Then after supper he rounded up all his professors and music experts and asked us to give them a little song.

*(She sings **Didn't It Rain**.)*

DIDN'T IT RAIN, CHILDREN, DIDN'T IT RAIN OH MY LORD.
DIDN'T IT, DIDN'T IT, DIDN'T IT, OH, MY LORD DIDN'T IT
    RAIN. *(repeat)*
IT RAINED FORTY DAYS, FORTY NIGHTS WITH-OUT
    STOPPING
NOAH WAS GLAD WHEN THE RAIN STOPPED DROPPING
A KNOCK AT THE WINDOW, A KNOCK AT THE DOOR
THEY CRIED, "OLD NOAH, WON'T YOU TAKE ONE MORE?"
NOAH CRIED OUT, "YOU'RE FULL OF SIN,
MY LORD'S GOT THE KEY AND YOU CAN'T COME IN!"
JUST LISTEN! HOW IT'S RAINING
JUST LISTEN! HOW IT'S RAINING
IN THE NORTH, IN THE SOUTH
IN THE EAST, IN THE WEST
ALL DAY, ALL NIGHT.
ALL NIGHT, ALL DAY.
OH TELL ME, DIDN'T IT RAIN CHILDREN, DIDN'T RAIN OH
    MY LORD.
DIDN'T IT, OH DIDN'T IT, DIDN'T IT, OH MY LORD, DIDN'T
    IT RAIN.

MAHALIA. *(cont.)* Well, as soon as we finished a great big fuss busted loose. Everybody began talking at once. The professors started arguing with each other and asking me all sorts of questions. *(to Music Inn audience stage left)* No…no…never had a lesson. Yes, that's right. Just singing in churches and gospel tents. Mmm? No, baby, ain't nobody taught me to sing no special way. I just found myself doing it. *(to audience)* Then they fussed all over again and got out a tape recorder and played some African bongo music and asked me if it sounded familiar. *(to Music Inn audience)* Well…I don't know nothing 'bout no jungle drums, but the beat sound good. Don't it sound good to you Mildred?

MILDRED. *(not quite sure what to say)* Oh, yes. That does something for me.

MAHALIA. Sure does. *(to audience)* Then they started buzzing all over again. *(to* **MILDRED***)* We into something with these crazy people! *(to audience)* Then Professor Stearns got up and asked me all about implied pulse, diatomic scale and overlapping antiphony. *(to God)* Jesus tender shepherd, don't leave me now! *(to Music Inn audience)* All you nice professors and PhDs are picking at my music like birds at a box of corn; telling me what my gospel music is made out of. Telling me it's jazz. Telling me it's blues. Telling me I'm singing twelve-twelve time when my foot knows it's four-four time. Now Halie going to tell you what gospel music is. It's good tidings. That's right, darlin's. Gospel music is good news in bad times. It's singing that comes from God telling us there's hope. It's a song of deliverance. A surrender of pain and suffering. It's a shout from the soul saying I am free at last. Free from slavery. Free from hate. Free from despair. Gospel is a song of joy so deep…that the world can hardly stand it.

MILDRED. Amen.

MAHALIA. *(to audience)* Then Mildred started playing "Down By The Riverside" *(***MILDRED** *does.)* and we all started singing and clapping and doing the holy dance. I tell you, I could have led all those music experts out the door, down to the lake, and they all have waded right in to be baptized. *(music out, phone starts ringing)* By the time Mildred and I drove back to Chicago everything started happening at once. It was like a dam broke. We weren't hardly unpacked when the phone started ringing.

MILDRED. *(on the phone)* Carnegie Hall!

MAHALIA. What you say?

MILDRED. Mr. Joe Bostic wants you to sing at Carnegie Hall in October! *(hands phone to* **MAHALIA***.)* Those music professors must be really talking you up.

MAHALIA. *(on the phone)* You must be some kind of fool, mister.

MILDRED. I'm not afraid to play Carnegie Hall.

MAHALIA. Hush, Mildred, one fool at a time! Listen, mister, do you know what you trying to do going into Carnegie Hall? My songs not high enough for Carnegie Hall. Carnegie Hall! That's for great opera singers.

MILDRED. Duke Ellington had a concert there three years ago.

MAHALIA. That's different; he's the daddy of 'em all. Duke Ellington is class. *(in the phone)* Now I don't know 'bout you, mister, but I am an authority on gospel, and they ain't got nothing like me and no gospel song at Carnegie Hall. Now if you'll excuse me...

MILDRED. This is a whole new audience, Mahalia. Who knows what will become of it.

MAHALIA. No! I say no!

MILDRED. The Lord is showing you a door if you got the sense to open it.

(MAHALIA covers the phone as she looks at MILDRED. She realizes there is no way out.)

MAHALIA. *(in the phone, barely audible)* All right, I'll do it.

MILDRED. Hallelujah!

MAHALIA. What you mean I won't be sorry? I'm already sorry now! *(slams phone down)*

MILDRED. *(pause)* What you going to wear?

MAHALIA. *(She gives MILDRED a look.)* Lord, why You put Halie up in Carnegie Hall?

MILDRED. I think you should come on with a looong train.

MAHALIA. Carnegie Hall scares me, Lord.

MILDRED. That's the way Marian Anderson did. *(with delight)* Oooo! Car-ne-gie Hall!

MAHALIA. *(with fear)* Oooo. Carnegie Hall. *(sits, then realizes)* We need an organ. *(rises)* Get Francis on the phone! Tell Mr. James Herbert Francis he going to play Carnegie Hall!

MILDRED. *(dialing)* Yes, ma'am.

MAHALIA. *(pacing)* The Lord is my light and my salvation; whom shall I fear? The Lord is the strength of my life; of whom shall I be afraid?

MILDRED. *(in the phone)* That's right, Francis, Carnegie Hall. It's a gospel breakthrough! Carnegie Hall. Hall. No, *Hall*! Car-ne-gie Hall!

(MAHALIA gives the audience a look.)

For the opera stars…?

(MAHALIA moans.)

It's a big deal, Francis; take my word for it.

(She hangs up as MAHALIA shakes her head in disbelief.)

MAHALIA. Call Bostic back. Tell him I don't want no orchestra. Orchestra like a girdle to me. *(MILDRED dials phone.)* And tell him we need a organ for Francis. And not a big pipe organ. Can't get no gospel out of a pipe organ, too grand. I want a Hammond organ. *(looking up)* Why would You do me like this, God? Has Halie displeased You? *(no answer)* You must be thinking my soul all loused up. *(She paces.)*

MILDRED. …That's right, a Hammond organ. And I'll need a nine foot ebony Steinway grand. That's right. Just like the Duke. *(She hangs up and imagines her fingers on that Steinway.)*

MAHALIA. *(Out front, in response to what she has just seen and heard.)* Lord have mercy. *(more pacing)* Though an host should encamp against me, my heart shall not fear.

(She suddenly stops and listens for a heartbeat, feeling her chest.)

I think it stopped. Mildred, my heart stopped! I can't breathe!

(To get more breathing room she hands MILDRED several rolls of money from her bosom. She catches her breath, gives MILDRED a suspicious look, then replaces the money. To audience.)

MAHALIA. *(cont.)* The Lord didn't end with Carnegie Hall either. That phone kept right on ringing. CBS wanted me for my very own radio show. Mitch Miller was after me to sign with Columbia Records as "The World's Greatest Gospel Singer." Concerts, tours, they even wanted Mahalia Jackson on television. Bing Crosby, Dinah Shore, Red Skel-e-ton, Arthur Godfrey...

MILDRED. *(just hanging up the phone)* Ed Sullivan!

MAHALIA. Ed Sullivan?

MILDRED. Ed Sullivan! He wants you for next Sunday night. "Mr. Broadway" going to put Mahalia Jackson in the living room of twenty million people! E-lec-tronic integration. Can't be nothing but the Lord's work.

MAHALIA. Call Francis! Tell that man to get his fingers over here now! Ed Sullivan Sunday night, Carnegie Hall only six months away! We need to rehearse!

(Blackout. The lights come up downstage center as she moves to the audience.)

Oh, I was hot. But you got to be strong to take popularity, oooh yes. Louis Armstrong was calling wanting me to come and sing the blues; saying I'm "Bessie Smith plus two." I told him I ain't studying 'bout no blues. What I have to say, I say in gospel. Halie got something give her by God and she ain't messing with it. "Fatha" Hines telling me to do something with my voice. Man, I'm doing something right now. I'm praising the name of Jesus. I hope to bring people to God with my singing. Night clubs waving ten thousand dollars a week at me. Won't catch Halie singing in no nightclub pleasure house, nooo sir! How can I sing the Lord's song in a strange land? And the newest "entertainment" craze. Gospel nightclubs. Doorman dressed up in a choir robe and halo. Scantily dressed waitresses taking your drink order wearing angel wings. Gospel turned into a show for nightclub drinkers to laugh and carouse to, making a mockery of God's work. Nooo, not going happen that way with Halie. Men and women have given their lives! You don't want people to blaspheme. *(looking up to God)* Lord, You know Halie a sinner. Sometimes I gets evil just like anybody. But You saved me, Lord, and washed me clean. And You not ashamed of Halie. And precious Lord Jesus, Halie not ashamed of You.

*(**MAHALIA** sings **I'm Going To Live The Life I Sing About In My Songs**.)*

I'M GOING TO LIVE THE LIFE I SING ABOUT IN MY SONGS.
I'M GOING TO STAND FOR RIGHT, ALWAYS SHUNNING THE
    WRONG.
IF I'M IN A CROWD, IF I'M ALONE,
ON THE STREETS OR IN MY HOME.
I'M GOING TO LIVE THE LIFE I SING ABOUT IN MY SONGS.
EVERY DAY, EVERY WHERE,
ON THE CROWDED THOROUGHFARE.
FOLKS MAY WATCH ME, FOLKS MAY SPOT ME,
SAY I'M FOOLIN' BUT I DON'T CARE.
I CAN'T GO TO CHURCH, SHOUT ALL DAY SUNDAY.
GO OUT AND GET DRUNK, RAISE HELL ON MONDAY.
I'M GOING TO LIVE THE LIFE I SING ABOUT IN MY SONGS.
NOT FOR GOLD, NOT FOR FAME,
BUT FOR THE LOVE OF JESUS' NAME.
I MUST ALWAYS WALK THE STRAIGHT AND NARROW WAY.
JESUS TOLD ME IN THAT DAY,
HE WILL WASH ALL MY SINS AWAY.
I'M GOING TO LIVE THE LIFE I SING ABOUT IN MY SONGS,
    SURE 'NUFF.

(Lights fade to black. The cyc changes and lights come up in center area.)

MILDRED. *(enters from right with "Carnegie" suitcase)* Great gettin' up day in the morning! A full house, Mahalia! Bostic says people lined up half way 'round the block for tickets, but Carnegie Hall is sold out!

MAHALIA. Get Francis! Bring him over here to the dressing room; it's five minutes 'til curtain.

*(She starts **MILDRED** off towards left and starts to pace.)*

MILDRED. *(back again)* Midtown traffic is all tied up. Sold out!

MAHALIA. *Will you go get Francis?*

(**MILDRED** *exits left as* **MAHALIA** *paces.*)

I'm scared, Lord. Scared these people will ruin me, what I already accomplished. *(stops)* Can You hear me, Lord? *(She listens.)* I can't hear You. Please, Lord, say something. Just whisper in Halie's ear. *(She paces some more.)*

(**MILDRED** *enters from left with* **FRANCIS** *who is holding onto her arm. He is blind and wears dark glasses. She seats him in left chair.)*

MILDRED. The house is packed, eight thousand people. They seating some on stage.

MAHALIA. I feel sick.

FRANCIS. Uh oh.

(**FRANCIS** *laughs. He thinks everything is funny, especially* **MAHALIA**.)

MILDRED. Bostic say all the critics here too. Ed Sullivan, Walter Winchell…everybody.

MAHALIA. *(panic is setting in)* I don't have no voice. My voice like a little bird.

FRANCIS. Lord, keep your eye on that little ol' sparrow there. He heee.

MILDRED. Belafonte is here too.

MAHALIA. *(struggling for air)* My heart is pounding. Feel like Count Basie playing in there. Ooooh! *(She collapses in right chair.)*

MILDRED. Oooooooh! *(She collapses in center chair.)*

FRANCIS. Why you moaning, Mildred? You ain't got to sing. He heee.

MILDRED. *(She rises, almost hysterical.)* Carnegie Hall! Do you know what that means, Francis? Do you? Caruso, Marian Anderson, Paul Robeson, Toscanini! Those are the people who have stepped inside the magic circle! Did you know they call it the magic circle? *Did you?* (**FRANCIS** *laughs.)* 'Course you didn't!

MAHALIA. Lord have mercy. They going to put a woman up to sing in Carnegie Hall can't read a note big as a car. *(***FRANCIS** *he heees.)*

MILDRED. That never had any training. *(She looks at **MAHA-LIA**, aghast.)* You not ready!

MAHALIA. *(rising up thunder)* What you mean I'm not ready? When David sang his psalms did he have any training? Mmm? When little David played on his harp did he read music? Did he? When the birds sing do they read music?

MILDRED. No, no, not that, nooo! You not dressed!

*(***MAHALIA** *shrieks and there is a mad scramble to find* **MAHALIA***'s suitcase.* **FRANCIS** *laughs. They find the suitcase. There is a struggle with it, and each other, as they try to get it open. The suitcase finally bursts open and several thousand dollars spill out.)*

MAHALIA. Mildred! Look what you done did. Pick up my money, you hear? Pick up all my money!

*(***FRANCIS** *is immediately on the floor gathering money.)*

Francis!! You sit your blind self down!

FRANCIS. Hee hee.

MAHALIA. Ain't none of that cash money going astray! *(Snatches money from **FRANCIS**.)*

STAGE MANAGER. *(from dressing room speaker)* Places, Miss Jackson.

MAHALIA. Lordy, help us make it to Jordan.

*(***MILDRED** *quickly retrieves a beautiful black velvet gown, with white trim and long train, from under the money. She holds the gown for **MAHALIA** to step in, as she kicks large stacks of money out of her way. They have great difficulty getting all of **MAHALIA** into the gown.)*

MAHALIA. Francis, I'm lucky you can't see this! *(more difficulty)* Francis, you lucky you can't see this!

STAGE MANAGER. Miss Jackson to the stage, please!

MAHALIA. All right!

*(The gown is zipped up now. **MILDRED** shovels the remaining money back into the suitcase and shuts it tight.)*

MAHALIA. *(cont.)* Hurry! Take Francis out.

*(***FRANCIS*** *takes* **MILDRED***'s arm and they exit left.*
MAHALIA *looks around and finds a few stray bills and
stuffs them down her front. She points an accusing
finger at someone in the front row.)*

You got any my money? Let me see your pockets. *(Still
not satisfied, but looking up now.)* Lord, this is it. I got to
go now. Mr. Bostic got my name in the paper and I got
to go. I'm vexed and sorry that man did this thing but
I'm a determined woman, You know that, and if I flop
I like to flop big. So I'm going on out there, Lord. Just
help me get through it.

*(She starts to exit, then returns for the suitcase, taking
a long suspicious look at the front row. She exits Left as
the lights fade. There is a transition of colors in the cyc.
We hear* **FRANCIS** *at the organ and* **MILDRED** *on piano.
The "magic circle" slowly comes up Center as* **MAHALIA**
*enters. She takes a deep breath, then steps into the spot-
light. She looks up to God, then closes her eyes and sings*
A City Called Heaven *with beauty and dignity.)*

I AM A POOR PILGRIM OF SORROW
AND I'M LEFT IN THIS WHOLE WIDE WORLD ALONE, ALONE
I HAVE NO HOPE FOR TOMORROW
BUT I'M TRYING TO MAKE HEAVEN MY HOME
WELL, SOMETIMES I'M TOSSED, LORD, AND I'M DRIVEN
SOMETIMES I DON'T KNOW WHICH WAY I CAN RUN
BUT I'VE HEARD OF A CITY CALLED HEAVEN
AND I'M STRIVIN' TO MAKE HEAVEN, LORD, MY HOME

*(The "magic circle" fades and there is a change in the
cyc. The area lights comes up as* **MAHALIA** *moves downstage center to audience.)*

When I got out there and stood in that magic circle
and thought about all those great stars standing where
I was, I got cold chills. Sweat started poppin' off me
big as a nickel. *(pointing up to God)* Then my daddy
whispered to me and I opened my mouth and sang
"A City Called Heaven." And baby, it's a doxology

in there. Then I started working it up with some of those bounce songs. People died, they screamed, they walked the floor. Some got up to dance in the aisles, tears streaming down their faces. I just lost sight of the people and sang. Guess I got a little carried away too. Ended up singing on my knees. They never seen that in Carnegie Hall.

(She removes robe as **MILDRED** *enters from left with* **FRANCIS.***)*

MILDRED. Glory hallelujah! Bostic says we broke the house record! Had more people than Benny Goodman or Toscanini!

(She seats **FRANCIS** *in left chair.)*

FRANCIS. He heee.

MILDRED. And listen to these reviews! *New York Times. (reading)* I thought I had confronted a Cecil B. De Mille mob scene when I reached Carnegie. And inside, an excited crowd wouldn't sit in their seats. Gospel moved to Carnegie Hall last night and the coming together was astonishing.

FRANCIS. He ain't said nothin' but the truth. He hee.

*(***MAHALIA** *calmly sits, holding Carnegie robe reverently in her lap.)*

MILDRED. Listen! Walter Winchell. *(reading)* Carnegie Hall was packed last night to hear Mahalia Jackson. You never heard of Mahalia Jackson? She's merely the world's greatest Gospel canary.

FRANCIS. I thought she was a little ol' sparrow. He heee.

MILDRED. Here's the last. *(reading)* Mahalia Jackson, the diva of gospel singers, was electrifying last night. Some inner spiritual force has given her the power to tell a story in song with as much passion and rapture as any prima donna who ever graced the stage. A genius unspoiled! A great artist! She can grace the most imperial concert hall in the world!

FRANCIS. That's right. 'cause she was up there singing with God. Singing with God. He heee.

MAHALIA. *(looking up)* Lord. Lord. Get Your glory.

(She rises and crosses downstage center as she sings How I Got Over.)

HOW I GOT OVER, HOW DID I MAKE IT OVER?

OH, MY SOUL LOOKS BACK AND WONDERS, HOW I MADE IT OVER.

HOW I MADE IT OVER, LAWD, COMIN' ON OVER ALL THESE YEARS?

YOU KNOW, MY SOUL LOOKS BACK AND WONDERS, HOW I MADE IT OVER.

BUT AS SOON AS I CAN SEE JESUS, THE MAN THAT MADE ME FREE.

THE MAN THAT BLED AND SUFFERED,

YOU KNOW HE DIED ON CALVARY'S TREE.

AND I WANNA THANK HIM FOR HOW HE'S BROUGHT ME.

AND I WANNA THANK HIM FOR HOW HE'S TAUGHT ME.

I WANNA THANK HIM FOR HOW HE'S KEPT ME.

YOU KNOW HE'S NEVER, NEVER, EVER, LEFT ME.

I WANNA THANK HIM FOR HIS HOLY BIBLE.

I WANNA THANK HIM FOR OLD TIME REVIVAL

AND I'M GONNA THANK HIM FOR OLD TIME RELIGION.

I WANNA THANK HIM FOR GIVING ME VISION.

AND I WANNA SING AROUND GOD'S ALTAR

AND I'M GONNA SHOUT, "ALL MY TROUBLES OVER."

YOU KNOW, I WANNA THANK YOU, THANK YOU FOR BEING SO GOOD TO ME.

HOW I MADE IT ON OVER, LORD.

I HAD TO CRY COMIN' ON OVER,

YOU KNOW MY SOUL LOOKS BACK IN WONDER HOW I MADE IT OVER.

I TELL YOU HOW I MADE IT OVER, LORD.

I HAD TO CRY COMIN' ON OVER.

YOU KNOW, MY SOUL LOOKS BACK IN WONDER HOW I MADE IT OVER.

(Lights fade to just the downstage center area.)

I WANNA THANK YOU THIS EVENING. I WANNA THANK YOU THIS EVENING.

GOD TOLD HIS ANGELS, GOD SAID, "TOUCH HER IN MY
    NAME!"
GOD SAID, "TOUCH HER IN MY NAME!"
I ROSE THIS MORNIN'. I ROSE THIS MORNIN'.
I FEEL LIKE SHOUTIN'. I FEEL LIKE SHOUTIN'.
I JUST GOTTA THANK GOD.
YOU KNOW I WANNA THANK YOU, THANK YOU FOR BEING
    SO GOOD TO ME.

(When **MAHALIA** *starts to shout, all lights fade except
the magic circle. She ends singing on her knees tears
streaming down her face. She is up there singing with
God again. The magic circle fades as the curtain falls.)*

End of Act I

ACT II

(As the house lights go down, we hear **MILDRED** *playing a traditional version of* **We Shall Overcome***. The curtain rises. Near the end of the music,* **MAHALIA** *enters from right and crosses to stage right limbo area. She reads from her Bible which is opened to Exodus.)*

MAHALIA. And Moses came to the mountain of God. And the angel of the Lord appeared unto him in a flame of fire, out of the midst of a bush: and he looked and behold, the bush burned with fire, and the bush was not consumed.

KING. *(lights come up on podium, stage left limbo area)* I am convinced that the universe is under the control of a loving purpose, and that in the struggle for righteousness, man has cosmic companionship.

MAHALIA. *(from Bible)* And Moses said, I will now turn aside and see this great sight, why the bush is not burnt.

KING. An all-loving God, who forever works through history for the establishment of His kingdom.

MAHALIA. And when the Lord saw that he turned aside to see, God called unto him out of the midst of the bush, and said, Moses, Moses. And he said, here am I.

KING. And when God calls, we must be willing to be co-workers with Him. God and man, made one in unity of purpose.

MAHALIA. And God said, "The place whereon thou standest is holy ground."

KING. Consecrated. Every human life a reflection of divinity, molded in the image of God.

MAHALIA. I am the God of thy Father. The God of Abraham, the God of Isaac, the God of Jacob.

KING. The God of love.

MAHALIA. And the Lord said, I have surely seen the affliction of my people which are in Egypt.

KING. And love shall implement the demands of justice.

MAHALIA. And I have heard their cry by reason of their taskmasters; for I know their sorrows.

KING. For every act of injustice mars and defaces the image of God in man.

MAHALIA. And I am come down to deliver them out of the hand of the Egyptians, and to bring them out of that land unto a good land.

KING. And all men and women, of all races and creeds, shall live together in peace and harmony, as brothers and sisters in the Beloved Community.

MAHALIA. A land flowing with milk and honey.

KING. The Kingdom of God come to earth.

MAHALIA. Come now, therefore, and I will send thee unto Pharaoh, that thou mayest bring forth my people out of Egypt.

(Lights fade stage left limbo as **MLK** *exits left.* **MAHALIA** *closes her Bible and sings the "Mahalia" version of **We Shall Overcome**.)*

WE SHALL OVERCOME,
WE SHALL OVERCOME,
WE SHALL OVERCOME SOME DAY

OH, DEEP IN MY HEART
I DO BELIEVE THAT
WE SHALL OVERCOME SOME DAY.

(from Bible) The prophet that hath a dream, let him tell his dream; and he that hath my word, let him speak my word faithfully, saith the Lord. *(to audience)* Martin Luther King Jr. had a dream…and he spoke in tongues of fire.

KING. *(lights up on podium, stage left limbo)* On this seventeenth day of May 1954, there is a great light of hope for millions of disinherited people. The United States

Supreme Court has declared segregation in this country's public schools, unconstitutional. We have left Egypt. God has parted the Red Sea and the forces of justice are moving to the other side.

MAHALIA. Jim Crow was dead now. And America waited, wondering how much the funeral was going to cost. In 1955 Mrs. Rosa Parks was brought to trial in Montgomery, Alabama for refusing to move out of her seat in the Negro section of the city bus so a white man could sit down. This was the spark that set fire to a mighty conflagration.

KING. There comes a time when people get tired. Tired of being mistreated, tired of being segregated and humiliated, tired of being kicked about by the brutal feet of oppression. But we cannot solve these problems with violence.

MAHALIA. The Montgomery Improvement Association was formed.

KING. We must meet hate with love. For the old law of an eye for an eye leaves everybody blind.

MAHALIA. The association elected Martin Luther King president...

KING. The only weapon in our hands will be the weapon of protest.

MAHALIA. ...and leader of a bus boycott.

KING. And if we protest with Christian love, history will pause and say, "There lived a great people. A black people, whose dignity and courage injected new meaning into the veins of civilization." This is our challenge and our overwhelming responsibility.

MAHALIA. And fifty thousand Negroes stepped off segregated buses...and fifty thousand Blacks started walking.

KING. For God has decided to use Montgomery Alabama as the proving ground for the struggle and triumph of freedom and justice in America.

(Lights out as **KING** *exits left.)*

MAHALIA. And empty buses travelled the streets of Montgomery...for almost a year. Then we got a call.

MILDRED. *(covering mouthpiece of phone)* It's Dr. King! They're having a rally to honor Mrs. Parks and raise a little money for the boycott. He wants to know if you might come down and sing. Says they need some inspiration.

MAHALIA. *(taking phone from* **MILDRED***)* We would be pleased to come down there and sing a little gospel.

MILDRED. We would?

MAHALIA. *(to* **MILDRED***)* Yes, we would.

(on phone as **MILDRED** *gets luggage from off right)*

What...*fee?* Honey, I ain't coming to Montgomery to make no money off them walkin' folks. *(hangs up phone)* So...Mildred and I drove on down. *(She sets two chairs downstage center.)*

MILDRED. *(She is a bundle of nerves as she enters with two suitcases and Mahalia's purse. She puts the luggage in the "trunk," hands purse to* **MAHALIA***, and sits behind the wheel.)* What you getting me into now? Going get me killed. Killed!

MAHALIA. *(She slams the trunk, then slides into the passenger seat, exhausted.)* These shoes is murder!

MILDRED. Don't say murder.

MAHALIA. *(She kicks off her shoes and lets out a sigh of relief.)* Ahhh.

MILDRED. Going get me carved up, I know it.

*(***MILDRED** *starts the car, puts it in gear and starts to drive off.* **MAHALIA** *finds a pair of Indian moccasins in her purse, puts them on, and holds her feet up for* **MILDRED** *to see.)*

MAHALIA. Now I'm just like those walkin' folk in Montgomery. My feets is tired but my "soles" at rest. Hah!

(She looks over to see if **MILDRED** *has enjoyed her little joke. She hasn't.)*

MILDRED. Shouldn't even be going, so much work to do. Letters to write, contracts to sign. Mitch Miller calling every other day wanting to know when you can record.

MAHALIA. Mr. Mitch Miller. Always trying to slick me up. Wants me to record something new besides gospel. Say he wants to "broaden me," make my records more popular. Well baby, there ain't nothing more popular than God. God is the most popular person there is. And Mitch honey…He loves you too.

MILDRED. Well, all that don't matter none 'cause we going be dead soon. *(looks over at* **MAHALIA***)* I wish I had nerves like you. Sit there like tomorrow never come and me so scared my hands about to shake right off this steering wheel.

MAHALIA. Ain't no need for me to be scared, miss. You enough for two.

MILDRED. *(close to tears now)* I am scared.

MAHALIA. *(gently)* Mildred, honey, we going down to Montgomery for a few days and help those poor walkin' people forget their feet hurt. Now, say your prayers and drive nice and easy, 'cause if a policeman stop us he won't never forgive me for owning this car.

MILDRED. I will.

MAHALIA. *(looking over to* **MILDRED***, then up to God)* Lord, we can't let Mildred know Halie scared too.

(The lights fade as they drive on.)

(Lights come up on **KING** *at podium, stage left limbo.* **MILDRED** *strikes luggage to right.* **MAHALIA** *puts heels back on and sets chairs for church scene.)*

KING. We must face our fears and master them with courage and faith. For God is able. And He shall lead us out of the wilderness and into the Promised Land. And we shall taste the milk of freedom and the honey of equality. *(exit left)*

MAHALIA. When we got to Montgomery The Reverend Ralph Abernathy had us to stay with him and Juanita and they gave us their own beds so we could get a good night's sleep.

MILDRED. *(enter from right)* You call that a good night's sleep? Cars screeching past all night long. Hecklers hootin' and hollerin' filthy names. Phone ringing all hours with death threats.

MAHALIA. Devil don't never sleep.

MILDRED. And Juanita says last night was nothing. Says they really be out today.

MAHALIA. Trying to break up the rally.

MILDRED. This town got an ugly way to it.

MAHALIA. *(to audience)* The rally was eight o'clock at St. John's Methodist Church, the biggest church in Montgomery.

MILDRED. Methodists and Baptists under one roof. Lord, what wonders You have wrought.

MAHALIA. *(to audience)* Police were all over. Cars racing back and forth with people trying to make trouble.

MILDRED. *(to MAHALIA)* Feel like there might be bullets.

MAHALIA. *(to audience)* And the church was packed out. Had been since noon. Reverend Abernathy got up and prayed for victory in the boycott; then Dr. King spoke.

MILDRED. *(lights up on church podium, left of centerstage)* Look at him. He's just a boy.

MAHALIA. Twenty-six years old. Look like his pictures, those eyes reachin' in. *(sits)*

KING. I woke up this morning with my mind stayed on freedom.

CONGREGATION. Preach on!

KING. And I got on my walking shoes.

CONGREGATION. Speak! Speak!

KING. And I ain't gonna let nobody turn me around!

CONGREGATION. No, sir!

KING. 'Cause I'm not walking for myself.

CONGREGATION. Oh, no!

KING. I'm walking for my children and my grandchildren.

CONGREGATION. That's right!

KING. And we shall protest nonviolently and with love.

CONGREGATION. Oh, yes!

KING. 'Cause hate is too big a burden to bear.

CONGREGATION. Too big, sir!

KING. And we shall force this city, this nation, this world, to face its own conscience.

CONGREGATION. Lord knows.

KING. For this struggle is not between black and white.

CONGREGATION. Oh, no!

KING. But between good and evil.

CONGREGATION. That's it!

KING. And whenever good and evil have a confrontation… good will win!

CONGREGATION. Yes, it will! *(on their feet now)*

KING. So, I'm gonna keep on keepin' on!

MAHALIA. Glory hallelujah! Praise God! Amen!

(MAHALIA sings Keep Your Hand on The Plow as the congregation joins in.)

HOLD ON, HOLD ON, KEEP YOUR HAND ON THE PLOW, HOLD ON.

HOLD ON, HOLD ON, KEEP YOUR HAND ON THE PLOW, HOLD ON. FREEDOM MARCHERS, BOUND IN JAIL, GOT NO MONEY FOR TO GO THEIR BAIL. KEEP YOUR EYES ON THE PRIZE, HOLD ON. AIN'T BUT ONE THING THEY DONE WRONG,

BUT STAY IN SEGREGATION A DAY TOO LONG. KEEP YOUR EYE ON THE PRIZE, HOLD ON.

HOLD ON, HOLD ON, KEEP YOUR EYE ON THE PRIZE, HOLD ON.

HOLD ON, HOLD ON, KEEP YOUR EYE ON THE PRIZE, HOLD ON.

WANT TO GET TO FREEDOM LET ME TELL YOU HOW,
KEEP YOUR HAND TO THE GOSPEL PLOW.
KEEP YOUR EYE ON THE PRIZE, HOLD ON.
HOLD ON, HOLD ON, KEEP YOUR EYE ON THE PRIZE, HOLD
    ON.
HOLD ON, HOLD ON, KEEP YOUR EYE ON THE PRIZE, HOLD
    ON.

MAHALIA. *(to audience as actor sets chairs for Abernathy living room)* I tell you, that church went up. I mean we turned it out. People shouting and testifying. We didn't leave nothin' standing, not even dust! And the balm of God's gospel healing all wounds. Afterwards, we were back at the Abernathy's and Jaunita made us all a down-home dinner. Collard greens, ham hocks, corn bread, with peach cobbler for dessert.

*(It is after dinner now and the others are already sitting, exhausted. **MAHALIA** collapses in center chair. There is a pause.)*

That civil rights makes you hongry.

MILDRED. *(in a daze)* I aged.

MAHALIA. Food like that got suption, helps get all the noxion out.

KING. *(laughing)* Mahalia, your singing taught me something tonight.

MAHALIA. What's that, honey?

KING. The surest path to the soul is through the heart.

MAHALIA. I just glad I can serve, 'cause nobody need the music like those who make it.

KING. A voice like yours comes along but once a millennium.

MAHALIA. Now is the needed time. Don't you see, baby? That's not me, that's God...working His plan. And He won't stop 'til every Negro can be free. *(She rises and starts digging down her front.)* Now Martin, you got to keep this movement movin'. *(She hands several large rolls of money to **KING**.)* That's twenty thousand dollars. Unlock some jails and get those folks out. (**KING** *looks* *amazed.)* Oh don't worry, darlin', they's plenty more where that came from.

*(She pats her bosom, as **KING** looks even more amazed. The lights change and **MAHALIA** sets two chairs downstage center for car.)*

First thing next morning Mildred and I started back home to Chicago.

MILDRED. Hurry up, let's go! *(She rushes on from right, throws luggage in the trunk and gets in the car.)* Come on hurry!

MAHALIA. I move faster when you don't rush me. *(**MAHALIA** takes her own sweet time.)*

MILDRED. Hurry! *(**MAHALIA** is in the car now.)* Shut the door. *(**MILDRED** starts the car.)* Shut the door!

*(**MAHALIA** shuts the door as **MILDRED** "floors" it. **MAHALIA** is thrown back in her seat as the car screeches off.)*

Goodbye Montgomery!

MAHALIA. Anybody think you were a little fidgety back there, Mildred. *(to audience)* The next night, a bomb blew out the living room of the Abernathy house… and the bedroom where Mildred and I stayed. Nobody hurt.

*(The lights change as **MAHALIA** comes downstage center to audience. **MILDRED** resets chairs and strikes luggage and purse.)*

On November 13, 1956, the Supreme Court declared Alabama's state and local laws requiring segregation on buses, unconstitutional. After Montgomery, freedom became contagious. Dr. King preached the gospel of nonviolence as "sit-ins" spread all across the South at lunch counters, libraries, movie theaters, swimming pools, and beaches. And all the time, gospel singing was an ally, soothing the soul and giving power to the march toward freedom in America.

*(We hear **FRANCIS** on the organ and **MILDRED** on piano trying to play the "The Star-Spangled Banner" as the lights come up full on center area.)*

MAHALIA. *(cont.)* Francis! Francis!

(She knocks on the organ to get his attention. They stop playing.)

We got to get this and you not gettin' it!

FRANCIS. It be's that way sometimes. He hee.

MAHALIA. I got to wrestle this thing to get the substance. *(She removes suit jacket which remains off for the rest of the play.)*

MILDRED. Well here's the substance, B flat. *(She hits B flat several times.)*

MAHALIA. And Mildred, don't you go telling me how to sing "The Star-Spangled Banner."

FRANCIS. He hee.

MAHALIA. I been singing "Star-Spangled Banner" since I been in school.

MILDRED. Yeah, but how many times you sung it in Washington, D.C. at the gala celebration for President John F. Kennedy at his inaugural ball while the whole world watches on TV?

MAHALIA. They should have let us sing songs we had made our own thing and got some nice known person in the neighborhood to sing "The Star Spangled Banner."

FRANCIS. *(giving* **MAHALIA** *the needle)* Yeah! Maybe sing some song off your new album like "Danny Boy" or "Green Leaves Of Summer." That's our thing.

MAHALIA. You an evil man.

FRANCIS. *(more of the needle)* Ooo, Mitch Miller right! Those songs just perfect for you.

MAHALIA. There's a lot I'm up against, baby.

FRANCIS. Or how 'bout "Peace In The Valley?" Elvis got himself a million-seller with that song Prof. Dorsey wrote special for you, but you ain't even recorded it. He hee.

MAHALIA. That's the way it go. Elvis Presley got his million-seller but Columbia wants Mahalia Jackson to take Jesus' name out of the title of her songs?

FRANCIS. What!

MILDRED. *(to* **FRANCIS***, quoting Columbia)* For "commercial purposes."

MAHALIA. Want to strike out Jesus. I told them, and I'll go on telling 'em; I want to praise my Jesus.

FRANCIS. Amen!

MILDRED. So what's new? Columbia always trying to dominate God. But you still a legend. Gallup Poll say you one of the most admired women in the world.

MAHALIA. *(with a touch of sarcasm)* Yeah, I been knowing that. That's wonderful.

MILDRED. "Downbeat" just voted you world's most acclaimed vocalist.

MAHALIA. I don't want but one vote and that's from Jesus. *(looking up)* Lord, I'm sorry I got mixed up in Columbia's business; you know it's not mine.

MILDRED. Well, never mind Columbia's business, how 'bout getting back to America's business?

(She pointedly hits B flat several times for **MAHALIA***'s benefit, then starts to play "The Star-Spangled Banner" again. As the lights cross-fade, the music segues into* **Lift Every Voice And Sing***, the unofficial Black national anthem.* **FRANCIS** *removes dark glasses. Actor now places podium on platform upstage center along with three chairs then exits left.)*

MAHALIA. *(downstage center to audience)* America's business is freedom! And Martin Luther King became the conscience of America, its troubled soul, insisting that wrong be made right. Because God's will and the heritage of our nation demands it. And that demand was heard on televisions all across America. In Birmingham, Dr. King dropped to his knees in prayer as he was arrested for demonstrating without a permit. And America watched as the police slapped and kicked old men and young boys. And America watched as snarling police dogs attacked unarmed protesters. And America watched as fire hoses were turned on women and children, while on their knees praying. And America watched…and saw her own guilt. *(Music out.)* If Montgomery was the first battle in the war to end segregation, then Birmingham was the turning point. And The March On Washington was the climax. The great coming together. Two hundred and fifty thousand people from every corner of the country. Black and white marching arm and arm from the Washington Monument down Constitution Avenue to the Lincoln Memorial.

MILDRED. The day of Jubilee has come at last!

(She is looking out at the great crowd as she enters from right. She hands **MAHALIA** *her purse.)*

MAHALIA. Girl, I didn't think anybody show. Last night this town like the Russians was coming, everything closed up and people gone.

MILDRED. Afraid they'd be trouble. But look, people saying "good morning" and having fun. Like a church picnic. And black and white together. Together!

MAHALIA. Look like the human race took a day off being mean to each other.

MILDRED. Look! *(crosses to left)* There's Marlon Brando and Sammy Davis Jr.!

MAHALIA. Who Marlon Brando?

MILDRED. Give me your camera. I want to get some pictures.

MAHALIA. *(She digs in her purse for her "brownie" camera and gives it to* **MILDRED**.*)* Be sure you get one of Mr. Lincoln sitting there. *(She indicates the Lincoln Memorial upstage center.)*

MILDRED. Most times he looks sad, but he's smilin' today. *(She takes his photograph.)*

MAHALIA. All the big names from show business were there, but it was the little people that were the heroes.

*(***MILDRED*** takes a photo of the heroes.)*

MAHALIA. *(cont.)* A great nation that had risen up and were marching toward us, singing the old spirituals and church hymns. Carrying American flags.

MILDRED. There's Martin. Martin!

(She waves, then motions him to stand in front of Lincoln so she can get their photo together, then **MLK** *sits left of podium.)*

MAHALIA. Like the vision of Moses, the children of Israel coming out of the wilderness and heading over to the Promised Land.

MILDRED. You supposed to go first, then Martin will speak. *(She takes* **MAHALIA**'s *purse and sits far right chair on platform.)*

MAHALIA. Descendants of slaves coming to claim their rights as Americans.

*(**MAHALIA** crosses to podium and sings **I've Been Buked**, a cappella.)*

I'VE BEEN BUKED AND I'VE BEEN SCORNED
I'VE BEEN BUKED AND I'VE BEEN SCORNED
I'VE BEEN BUKED AND I'VE BEEN SCORNED
YOU KNOW, I'VE BEEN TALKED ABOUT SURE YOU BORN

I'M GONNA TELL MY LORDY WHEN I GET HOME
I'M GONNA TELL MY LORDY WHEN I GET HOME
I'M GONNA TELL MY LORDY WHEN I GET HOME, LORD
JUST HOW LONG THEY BEEN TREATING ME WRONG

*(**MAHALIA** sits right and **KING** rises and crosses to podium. He takes speech from jacket pocket and starts to read.)*

KING. Five score years ago, a great American, in whose symbolic shadow we stand today, *(indicates Lincoln behind him)* signed the Emancipation Proclamation. This momentous decree came as a joyous daybreak to end the long night of captivity for millions of slaves. But one hundred years later the Negro still is not free. One hundred years later…

MAHALIA. Tell 'em 'bout the dream, honey!

KING. *(He looks over at* **MAHALIA** *then puts away his paper and speaks from his heart.)* I say to you today, my friends, that even though we face the difficulties of today and tomorrow, I have a dream. *(moves downstage center to audience)* I have a dream that one day this nation will rise up and live out the true meaning of it's creed: "We hold these truths to be self-evident; that all men are created equal." I have a dream that one day, on the red hills of Georgia, sons of former slaves and the sons of former slave-owners will be able to sit down together at the table of brotherhood. I have a dream! I have a dream that my four little children will one day live in a nation where they will not be judged by the color of their skin but by the content of their character. And this will be the day when all God's children will be able to sing with new meaning, "My country 'tis of thee, sweet land of liberty, of thee I sing. Land where my fathers died, land of the pilgrim's pride, from every mountainside, let freedom ring." So let freedom ring. And all of God's children, black men and white men, Jews and Gentiles, Protestants and Catholics, will be able to join hands and sing in the words of that old Negro spiritual, "Free at last! Free at last! Thank God almighty, we are free at last!"

*(***KING*** *returns to podium as the crowd is applauding wildly. The lights change.* **MILDRED** *goes to piano and starts playing a very slow version of "Kum Ba Yah." Actor returns chairs from platform and replaces podium to downstage left limbo and exits left.)*

MAHALIA. *(moving downstage)* Then, just as quietly as they had come, the great crowd began to steal away. The last songs died away. And we left as we had come, with peace and goodwill toward all. *(music out)* But Satan gets mad when you try to do good and his hatred drove the sweetness out of the land. Good will died and peace fled down the road as the apostles of violence had their innings. Assassinations, riots, troubles.

MAHALIA. *(cont.)* White power! Black power! Everybody forgetting God power.

(MILDRED *slowly and softly plays* **Gonna Sing About Martin** *as* **MAHALIA** *crosses to stage right limbo and reads from her Bible.)*

And the Lord God appeared in a pillar of a cloud. And the Lord said unto Moses, Behold, thou shalt sleep with thy fathers; and this people shall forsake me, and break my covenant which I have made with them. Therefore, write ye this song and teach it the children of Israel: put it in their mouths that this song may be a witness for me. Moses, therefore, wrote this song the same day, and taught it the children of Israel.

KING. *(at podium, stage left limbo)* The Lord tests the righteous and the wicked.

MAHALIA. Give ear, O ye heavens, and I will speak.

KING. And His soul hates him that loves violence.

MAHALIA. Hear, O earth, the words of my mouth.

KING. The solution to the problems of this world…is love.

MAHALIA. My doctrine shall drop as the rain.

KING. The great unifying force of life…is love.

MAHALIA. My speech shall distil as the dew.

KING. The highest good…is love.

MAHALIA. And I will publish the name of the Lord.

KING. God…is love.

MAHALIA. Ascribe ye greatness unto our God.

KING & MAHALIA. *(together)* He is the rock.

MAHALIA. His work is perfect, for all His ways are judgment.

KING. Now the judgment of God is upon us.

MAHALIA. A God of truth.

KING. We must learn to live together as brothers and sisters.

MAHALIA. Just and right is God.

KING. Or we are going to perish together as fools.

MAHALIA. O that ye were wise, that ye understood this.

KING. We must learn to love.

MAHALIA. And Moses spake all the words of this song in the ears of the people. *(music out.)*

KING. I don't know what will happen now. We've got some difficult days ahead, here in Memphis.

MAHALIA. And the Lord spake unto Moses that selfsame day saying, get thee up into mount Nebo.

KING. But it really doesn't matter with me now...

MAHALIA. And the Lord showed him the land of Canaan.

KING. ...because I've been to the mountaintop.

MAHALIA. And the Lord said unto him, behold. This is the land I have promised unto the children of Israel.

KING. And I've looked over Jordan. And I've seen the Promised Land.

MAHALIA. But thou shalt not go over thither...

KING. I may not get there with you. But I want you to know, we as a people will get to the Promised Land.

MAHALIA. For thou shalt be gathered unto thy forefathers.

KING. And I'm happy tonight. I'm not worried about anything. I'm not fearing any man. *(looking up, hands extended)* Mine eyes have seen the glory of the coming of the Lord.

MAHALIA. And Moses, the servant of the Lord, died there in the land of Moab,

(The light on KING fades and goes out.)

according to the word of the Lord.

(Actor exits left with podium. MAHALIA crosses to center and sings Deep River.)

DEEP RIVER, MY HOME IS OVER JORDAN.
DEEP RIVER, LORD,
I WANT TO CROSS OVER INTO CAMPGROUND.
DEEP RIVER, MY HOME IS OVER JORDAN.
DEEP RIVER, LORD,
I WANT TO CROSS OVER INTO CAMPGROUND.
OH DON'T YOU WANT TO GO TO THE GOSPEL FEAST,

(She falls to her knees.)

THAT PROMISED LAND WHERE ALL IS PEACE?
DEEP RIVER, LORD,
I WANT TO CROSS OVER INTO CAMPGROUND.

MAHALIA. *(cont.)* And there arose not a prophet since like unto Moses, whom the Lord knew face to face.

(Center lights fade. There is a slow transition as the cyc lights go from near dark to bright blue.)

(All lights come up full. It's Sunday night church at Greater Salem.)

You all come back over to Greater Salem next Sunday night and let Halie cook you some of her fine New Orleans gumbo! We going have a time, a good time, a marvelous time in the Lord. And we going raise a little money for the Baptist Missionary School. Now babies, this going be a silent offering! That mean all that money you got that make noise you just keep and you bring Halie those nice quiet bills. Ha!

(The congregation continues to respond during the following build-up. **FRANCIS** *is singing and playing "response" on organ,* **MILDRED** *on piano.)*

Lord have mercy! I'm feelin' gooood! Now, everybody know Mildred here and Blind Francis.

(They give a little wave and the congregation starts to applaud. **MAHALIA** *holds up hands in protest.)*

Noo, no. We not here tonight for form and fashion or some outside show of this world. No, we here for church.

FRANCIS. Let the church roll on!

MAHALIA. And when I say church, I mean lowdown *chu'ch!* Ain't that right, Francis?

FRANCIS. Sister, you know the church my fillin' station! And I'm looking to be filled with the Holy Ghost tonight! He hee.

MAHALIA. Hallelujah! Now beloveds, I ain't got nothing new for you this evening. Same old Mahalia Jackson, same old Jesus.

MILDRED. That's all right.

MAHALIA. But baby darlin's, I'm not ashamed. 'Cause I ain't found nothin' better than Jesus. He's given me a song can't nobody sing but me! And I know what I know. I know He heals the sick and raises the dead.

FRANCIS. *(singing)* Dr. Jesus!

MAHALIA. And He's continually resurrected in the hearts of them that love Him.

MILDRED. Amen!

MAHALIA. So don't you be losing hope, 'cause God can still heal this mean old troubled land.

FRANCIS. God is able!

MAHALIA. I know this world is so confused and frustrated with things going on we ain't never seen before. But we mustn't become discouraged. We must go back to the Bible and remember what our fore-parents taught us. How good God is. And how God can make a way.

FRANCIS. Yes, He will!

MAHALIA. God's brought salvation!

MILDRED. Hallelujah!

MAHALIA. But you got to believe.

FRANCIS. Yes, you do!

MAHALIA. 'Cause this world going try and tell you that everybody who believe in God is dumb or ignorant.

FRANCIS. Uh oh!

MAHALIA. Well, you got to get educated 'bout God's ways and know for yourself. 'Cause you can go to college...

FRANCIS. *(singing and responding on organ)* You can go to college!

MAHALIA. ...you can go to school!

FRANCIS. *(again)* You can go to school!

MAHALIA. But you ain't got Jesus!

FRANCIS. *(again)* ...ain't got Jesus!

MAHALIA. You an educated fool!

FRANCIS. *(and again)* ...educated fool! (**FRANCIS** *finishes off with a final flourish on organ.*)

MILDRED. Amen!

MAHALIA. Ooo, I better shut up. I supposed be a singer not a preacher. Mildred, start us off. And you all make room there 'cause when I sing, I sings with everything... including my feet. 'Cause they been saved too!

*(She sings **Dig A Little Deeper** and the Holy Ghost descends. **MILDRED** gets off on piano and **FRANCIS** tears it up on organ. **MAHALIA** sings and shouts, rapt in her holy dance as she skips across the stage into the congregation and up the aisle. The spirit gets high and Greater Salem goes to glory with singing, clapping, and shouting.)*

NEARER TO THEE, I WANT TO BE, OH MY LORDY
I WANNA DIG A LITTLE DEEPER
IN THE STOREHOUSE OF HIS LOVE, ETERNAL LOVE
I WANT TO SHINE, WITH LOVE SUBLIME, OH MY LORDY
I WANNA DIG A LITTLE DEEPER
IN THE STOREHOUSE OF GOD'S LOVE
OH LORD, I WANNA DIG A LITTLE DEEPER

CONGREGATION.

DIG A LITTLE DEEPER

MAHALIA.

DIG A LITTLE DEEPER

CONGREGATION.

DIG A LITTLE DEEPER

MAHALIA.

DIG A LITTLE DEEPER
IN THE STOREHOUSE OF HIS LOVE, ETERNAL LOVE
I WANNA TALK MORE LIKE MY JESUS WOULD
AND WALK MORE LIKE A CHRISTIAN SHOULD
I WANNA DIG A LITTLE DEEPER
IN THE STOREHOUSE OF GOD'S LOVE

(repeat chorus)

(NOW LISTEN) I WANT TO DO, WHAT'S ALWAYS TRUE, OH MY LORDY
I WANNA DIG A LITTLE DEEPER IN THE STOREHOUSE OF GOD'S LOVE, ETERNAL LOVE

MAHALIA. *(cont.)*

    EACH PASSING HOUR, I WANT MORE POWER, OH MY LORDY
    I WANNA DIG A LITTLE DEEPER IN THE STOREHOUSE OF
      GOD'S LOVE

FRANCIS. Somebody here now, must be the Lord! *(He lets out a high pitched scream.)*

MILDRED. Hold on, Francis!

MAHALIA.

    OH LORD, I WANT TO DIG A LITTLE DEEPER

CONGREGATION.

    DIG A LITTLE DEEPER

MAHALIA.

    DIG A LITTLE DEEPER

CONGREGATION.

    DIG A LITTLE DEEPER

MAHALIA.

    DIG A LITTLE DEEPER IN THE STOREHOUSE OF HIS LOVE,
      ETERNAL LOVE
    TALK MORE LIKE MY JESUS WOULD
    WALK MORE LIKE A CHRISTIAN SHOULD
    DIG A LITTLE DEEPER IN THE STOREHOUSE OF HIS LOVE

(Greater Salem is in an uproar. **MAHALIA** *is shouting.* **FRANCIS** *is falling out. Finally, the storm passes over.)*

MAHALIA. You enjoyed yourselves, didn't you darlin's? *(She has difficulty recovering her breath.)* Whew, 'bout popped my girdle on that one. My my. I do pretty good for an old girl, don't I?

FRANCIS. You a song singin' thing! He hee.

MAHALIA. Lord have mercy! Now that's what I call *chu'ch!*

(blackout)

(Lights up on **MAHALIA,** *stage left limbo.)*

Lord, You spoke to me once and I didn't want to take it. Then You spoke a second time, saying, "You gonna need it." But I resisted. Then You spoke a third time. Clear. Clear. You said, "Go!" So I have to obey. I'm going home now and I'll buy two whole sections of plots at Providence Memorial. That's the best cemetery open to us.

(She goes to center chair as lights crossfade to center area.)

MILDRED. *(enters from right waving a contract and carrying glass of water)* London, Paris, Stockholm, Frankfurt, Berlin…a full European tour!

FRANCIS. William Morris Agency finally starting to earn their money. He hee.

MILDRED. *(gives water to* **MAHALIA.***)* And best of all, Mahalia, two weeks in the Holy Land!

MAHALIA. Jerusalem?

MILDRED. *(hands contract to* **MAHALIA***)* Tacked right on to the end of the tour!

MAHALIA. *(exhausted, looking at contract)* Lord, if You never bless me again You blessed me enough.

MILDRED. Oh, yes. They also wish me to advise you that a check made out to Miss Jackson for ten thousand dollars has been outstanding for nine months.

MAHALIA. It's all right. I got it right here in "First National Savings and No Loans." *(She pats her bosom.)* Reach me my purse there, baby.

MILDRED. Europe. *(hands purse to* **MAHALIA** *then sits)* Seem like gospel music dead in America. Died when Martin died. But they want you in Europe.

MAHALIA. It is dead here. Don't require good gospel singing here anymore. Young people have too many other "options." *(She digs in her purse and finds her pills.)*

MILDRED. Rock 'n Roll. Soul music.

MAHALIA. Gospel everything we needed.

MILDRED. Our all and all.

MAHALIA. *(sigh)* Old singers from another era, that's us. Brought up on nothin' but mother wit and Jesus. *(She takes pill with a drink of water.)*

MILDRED. *(sighing, deep in self-pity)* The spotlight don't stay on forever.

MAHALIA. We had some rare stuff though. We has-beens, but we good has-beens.

FRANCIS. Man, I'm going be sick. Has-beens! Gospel still the greatest music there is! It's the best! *(stands)* It's the best because it's about power and hope in the present. Music written out of people's burdens, not some sort of la-de-dah just to make money. All this new beat. *Soul music...*that got no power on the soul. *Rock 'n Roll* ...sound like little lost children. Listen, people always going ride the gospel train no matter what the world say 'cause no other music can transport you to higher ground like gospel. It's good news in hard times. And when times get hard, people always go back to the "Old Landmark." No, when there ain't no more gospel, there won't be no more nothin'. *(sits)*

MAHALIA. *(pause)* Well, amen. You done told it all, didn't you?

MILDRED. *(taking mock offence)* Really dished us out didn't he?

FRANCIS. Had to. 'Fraid I might have to go to Europe alone; walk the streets of Jerusalem by myself.

MILDRED. You not leaving me here while having yourself a time way over in Beulah!

MAHALIA. Lordy, Jerusalem! *(kissing William Morris contract)* That's the most important thing in my life, to walk the streets where our Jesus once walked.

*(She gets happy, waving contract about, and sings **Walk in Jerusalem** as the others join in.)*

LORD, I'M GONNA WALK IN JERUSALEM,
TALK IN JERUSALEM,
SING IN JERUSALEM,
BE IN JERUSALEM,
HIGH UP IN JERUSALEM WHEN WE "FLY."

MILDRED. *(stops singing)* Fly! What you mean, fly?

MAHALIA. *(still singing, making like an airplane)*
WAY UP, WAY UP, WAY UP,
HIGH UP IN JERUSALEM WHEN WE FLY.

MILDRED. Fly? You mean like in a airplane?

MAHALIA. *(singing)*
> WAY UP, WAY UP, WAY UP,
> HIGH UP IN JERUSALEM WHEN WE FLY.

MILDRED. We're not taking a boat? I thought we were taking a boat.

MAHALIA. Listen, Mildred, it's all right. I talked with my Aunt Duke and she say it's all right 'cause she talked with the Lord and it's all right for me to fly.

MILDRED. You talked to your aunt but I ain't talked to mine.

(MAHALIA and FRANCIS resume their singing.)

Your aunt told you to fly but my aunt didn't tell me nothin'!

MAHALIA. *(singing and dancing, trying to get MILDRED to join)*
> LORD KNOWS WE'RE GONNA BE IN JERUSALEM,
> SING IN JERUSALEM,
> SHOUT IN JERUSALEM,
> PRAY IN JERUSALEM,
> HIGH UP IN JERUSALEM WHEN WE FLY.

(MAHALIA's phone is ringing. MILDRED goes to answer it.)

MILDRED. Got to fly to Jerusalem on her aunt. *(on the phone)* Hello!

(FRANCIS and MAHALIA continue singing.)

It's Columbia. *(shouting)* It's Columbia!

(They stop singing.)

They want to record us "live" in Europe. *(into the phone)* I just hope we be "live" in Europe.

(She slams the phone down. Blackout. We hear the sound of a jet taking off as the cyc changes.)

MAHALIA. *(to audience as light come up downstage right center)* Our first stop was London. Six thousand people crammed into Albert Hall...royalty in the box! Every five minutes more and more flowers and big baskets of fruit was delivered to the dressing room. And the audience…they couldn't have been English. Cheering and clapping…and clapping correctly, on two and four. Not like some of y'all here. *(She points an accusing finger at a few in the audience.)* A standing ovation! They like to loved us to death.

FRANCIS. They think we the Beatles.

MAHALIA. Then off we went to Stockholm, then Copenhagen, then Paris.

MILDRED. I'm going buy some French lace.

MAHALIA. We brought the French to their feet too. People waving and crying, throwing tons of bouquets right onto the stage.

FRANCIS. I'm going take us to the finest restaurant in Paris with all white linen and all and we going order the fanciest thing on the menu; whatever we want. And there won't be nobody messin' with us saying we can't. He hee. *(pause)* Too bad can't none of us parlez vous no French.

MAHALIA. *(to audience)* Paris in the springtime. Riding down the Champs-Elysees.

MILDRED. *(pointing for Francis)* Look! There's the Eiffel Tower!

FRANCIS. Oooo! **(MILDRED** *gives him a playful slap on the shoulder.)* He hee.

MAHALIA. Lord, you brought Halie from the swamps of the Mississippi to the streets of Paris. Who wouldn't believe in a God like that? *(to audience)* On to Zurich, Munich, Heidelberg. Everywhere we go, like a down-home revival meeting. Hamburg!

MILDRED. Oooo they said Hamburg was for shopping. Look at that crystal! And the china…!

MAHALIA. Mildred, honey, look at there! That's that egg-shell porcelain china. That's the same just like Mrs. Plant used to scold Halie not to break when I'd help Aunt Duke wash up after their parties. I'm going buy two full sets. One for me and one for Aunt Duke. Hah! *(to audience)* We killed 'em dead in Hamburg; called us back for seven encores. *(seriously to* **MILDRED***)* Remind me to bill them for overtime. On to Berlin! *(She puts on a long dressy shawl from downstage left bench.)* Six thousand people at the Sportspalast going crazy. They wouldn't let me go; kept calling us back for more. Stomping their feet in unison saying Mah-hahl-ya! Mah-hahl-ya!. The place was rockin'! *(Music vamp.)* Looking to get scary! Lord, don't let those children come up on this stage! Keep playing, Francis, keep playing!

(She quickly hobbles right and collapses in downstage right chair, exhausted and in pain. **MILDRED** *is panicky.)*

MILDRED. You better get back out there and give 'em one more or there's gonna be a riot.

MAHALIA. *(out of breath)* See you can find my purse over there.

MILDRED. *(thinking the worst)* What's wrong? Do you need a pill?

MAHALIA. Just reach me my purse.

MILDRED. *(beside herself)* Is it your heart?

MAHALIA. No, Mildred, it's my feet! *(She kicks off her shoes.)*

MILDRED. *(relieved.)* Lordy! *(She hands her the purse.)*

MAHALIA. They just told me they ain't going another step in these here shoes!

*(***MAHALIA*** takes moccasins from her purse and starts to put them on.)*

MILDRED. You can't go out there like that!

MAHALIA. Honey, if I take my shoes off at the White House I can take 'em off here for the same reason…'cause my feet hurt!

(She goes back on stage as **MILDRED** *puts Mahalia's shoes in purse and goes to piano.)*

All right, all right. You make me feel like I'm a star. Now, I'll sing another for you if you don't mind Mahalia singing in her Indian moccasins she got at Wisconsin Dells. Here we go. *(She gets the audience snapping their fingers.)* Come on, now. Ooo, that's nice.

*(She sings **Elijah Rock**.)*

MAHALIA.

ELIJAH ROCK. SHOUT! SHOUT! SHOUT!
ELIJAH ROCK. COMING OF THE LORD.
ELIJAH ROCK. SHOUT! SHOUT! SHOUT!
ELIJAH ROCK. COMING OF THE LORD.

ELIJAH! ELIJAH! ELIJAH!

SATAN IS A LIAR AND A CONJURER TOO
HE DON'T MIND HOW HE CONJURES YOU
IF I COULD I SURELY WOULD
I'D STAND ON THE ROCK THAT MOSES STOOD

(CHORUS)

YOU CAN CALL MY ROCK IN THE MORNING
CALL HIM LATE AT NIGHT
HE'S ALWAYS WITH ME
ALL MY BATTLES HE WILL FIGHT
WHEN I'M IN TROUBLE I CAN CALL HIM ON THE LINE
HE PUT A TELEPHONE IN MY HEART
AND I CAN CALL GLORY ANY TIME, HALLELUJAH!

(CHORUS)

(after song) Thank you, babies.

*(She takes a bow and throws some kisses. **FRANCIS** plays the chorus of **Down By The Riverside**, Mahalia's closer.)*

Oh my me, they's coming! They's coming up on stage! Mildred, we in trouble!

MILDRED. *(frozen in fear)* Lord, put out your mantle, we gonna be killed!

MAHALIA. Quick, get Francis! The limousine at the stage door! **(MILDRED** *runs to* **FRANCIS.)** Don't you come up here! No, sir, you stay right there! *(singing)*

MAHALIA AIN'T GONNA SING NO MORE.
MAHALIA AIN'T GONNA SING NO MORE.
MAHALIA AIN'T GONNA SING NO MORE.
MAHALIA AIN'T GONNA SING NO MORE.

(MILDRED *has* **FRANCIS** *and is heading off right.)*

MAHALIA. No, girl, the other way! The other way! *(singing)*
MAHALIA AIN'T GONNA SING NO MORE…(ETC.)
FRANCIS. Feet, do your duty!

(They run left and quickly pile into the waiting limousine as MAHALIA covers their retreat; waving and bowing and throwing kisses.)

MAHALIA. Oh, you just too good to Halie! Bye! *(She dashes to the limousine.)*

MILDRED. Lock the doors! Lock the doors! *(They do.)* Go man, go!

(She hits the driver a few times in her excitement and they drive off. They burst out laughing.)

MAHALIA. Europe done made me glad twice. Glad to come and glad to go. *(She puts "Elijah" scarf in purse.)*

*(**FRANCIS** starts to sing **I'm on my Way**. **MILDRED** and **MAHALIA** join in. The mood is high.)*

FRANCIS.

I'M ON MY WAY TO CANAAN LAND,
I'M ON MY WAY TO CANAAN LAND,
I'M ON MY WAY TO CANAAN LAND,
I'M ON MY WAY, GLORY HALLELUJAH, I'M ON MY WAY.

*(The lights on the limousine dim as **MAHALIA** rises and crosses to stage left limbo. **FRANCIS** continues to sing underneath Mahalia's speech. Softly, in a whisper. The tempo is slower now, more like a hymn. **MILDRED** sings along with him, as in a lullaby.)*

MAHALIA. Lord, You been so good to me. You have never forsaken me. Last night I saw myself in my coffin, no mistaking. I looked up and the lid was closing down. I just want to know, Lord…are You going to be with me in the shadows of death? *(singing with the others)*
I'M ON MY WAY, GLORY HALLELUJAH, I'M ON MY WAY.

(fade)

MILDRED. *(lights up full)* Damascus, Galilee, Jericho, Bethlehem. Not one inch of ground that's not in the Bible! All the places you been singing about since you a little girl in the choir at Mt. Moriah.

(She hands purse to **MAHALIA,** *which she carries throughout the Holy Land.)*

MAHALIA. Never dreamed these poor eyes would see the glory. God is real. I'm ready for the pilgrimage! Got me my walking shoes. *(She shows the others her moccasins.)*

FRANCIS. Going march right on up to Zion! He hee.

(He takes **MILDRED***'s arm.)*

MAHALIA. *(to audience)* There's a stone that marks where the manger stood in Bethlehem.

MILDRED. *(pointing downstage center)* There it is.

MAHALIA. It's a church here now, Francis.

(She kneels. He takes his hat off.)

MILDRED. This is where Jesus was born.

(With **MILDRED***'s help,* **FRANCIS** *puts his hand on the stone.)*

MAHALIA. Mary's tiny baby. What wonders You have wrought.

MILDRED. Just think. This is where the shepherds came to worship the newborn King. *(to* **MAHALIA***)* This is where the angels sang praises to His name.

MAHALIA. The first gospel singers…announcing the good news.

FRANCIS. Peace on earth. Good will toward men.

*(***FRANCIS** *and* **MILDRED** *help* **MAHALIA** *up.* **FRANCIS** *takes* **MILDRED***'s arm as they move downstage right.)*

MAHALIA. *(to audience)* It surprised me. The River Jordan is a little river. It runs fast, but not very deep. *(looking around)* Jesus was baptized near this very spot.

(She kneels. **FRANCIS** *is standing left of her;* **MILDRED** *Right.)*

MAHALIA. *(cont.)* It's muddy brown, just like the Mississippi in New Orleans. *(closing her eyes, remembering)* Lord, I can see Halie dressed all in baptism white. And I see all the saints standing behind me singing.

*(They sing **Let us Go Down to Jordan**.)*

LET US GO DOWN TO JORDAN
LET US GO DOWN TO JORDAN
LET US GO DOWN TO JORDAN
RELIGION IS SO SWEET

MAHALIA. I pray for another rebirth, Lord. Closer to the image of Your righteousness.

(She starts to dip hand into the Jordan, stops, and helps **FRANCIS.** *They all dip their hands.)*

FRANCIS. Feels cool.

MILDRED. Mmmm.

*(***MILDRED** *helps* **FRANCIS** *to his feet and they both help* **MAHALIA.** *They cross to center,* **FRANCIS** *on* **MILDRED** *'s arm.)*

MAHALIA. *(to audience)* Gethsemane was fragrant with the smell of flowers.

*(***FRANCIS** *inhales deeply.* **MAHALIA** *looks around.)*

This is where our Lord's spirit suffered so. This is where He was betrayed.

MILDRED. Look at these olive trees.

*(***FRANCIS** *reaches out front to touch.* **MILDRED** *helps.)*

Some of these trees over two thousand years old.

FRANCIS. Twisted with His agony.

MAHALIA. *(moving downstage left then pointing out front)* Look! The city of David. *(taking it all in)* That high part is where Solomon built the temple.

MILDRED. Our eyes looking over just like Jesus did. "O Jerusalem, Jerusalem!"

FRANCIS. "Glorious things are spoken of thee, O City of God."

MAHALIA. *(to audience)* The streets are cobbled-stone and narrow in Old Jerusalem.

(MAHALIA moves slowly upstage center; the stones hurting her feet. MILDRED helps FRANCIS.)

MILDRED. *(to FRANCIS)* This is the "Via Dolorosa." ...that means "Way of Sorrows."

MAHALIA. This is where Jesus carried the cross. *(looking around)* These walls heard the mockery as He stumbled. *(to audience)* At the top of the way is the Church of the Holy Sepulcher.

(She hobbles slowly, coming straight downstage center)

FRANCIS. When we going start up to Calvary?

MILDRED. We're on Calvary now, Francis.

(FRANCIS nods and takes his hat off.)

MAHALIA. *(to audience)* Inside there's a small marble chapel and candles flicker all around a golden altar. Under the altar is a recessed place in the stone. *(They kneel.)*

MILDRED. *(whispering to FRANCIS)* This is the tomb where Jesus was laid.

FRANCIS. *(to MAHALIA, as she weeps)* "Ye seek Jesus, which was crucified. He is not here, for He is risen!"

MAHALIA. Thank You, Jesus. Thank You, Jesus. Thank You, Jesus.

(MILDRED puts her arm around MAHALIA. FRANCIS is on the opposite side of MAHALIA. She reaches over and takes his hand. After a moment, MILDRED and FRANCIS help MAHALIA to her feet. They step back from the altar. She has recovered now.)

I hate to leave. Jerusalem been my coming home.

MILDRED. Better be coming home to Chicago, been gone too long.

FRANCIS. Seven weeks.

MAHALIA. Satan probably sittin' in my living room watching my new color TV. Havin' himself a time. Havin' himself a time.

*(They start to leave, as the lights fade. **MILDRED** goes to the piano and **FRANCIS** to the organ. We hear the final notes of the **Star-Spangled Banner** coming from Mahalia's TV as the center lights come up on **MAHALIA** sitting in her Chicago living room.)*

TV ANNOUNCER. This is WBBM-TV Channel 2, Chicago. We will resume programming...

*(**MAHALIA** takes remote from her purse and turns off the TV.)*

MAHALIA. Lord, You brought Halie from a mighty long way. Yes, You did. My soul look back in wonder. Mercy! In just the lift of Your eyebrow. A little barefoot girl in Loosiana coming down the track picking up coal, bringing it home, putting it in the bin. No more school now, uh uh! Halie pulled from the third grade. Got to tend family; take care of the little sweet babies. Sweep and dust every day, scrub the floors every second day. Except Sunday. Sunday, that's the day! Got to stick with the Lord! Church the best! *(singing)* Han me down. Han me down yo' silver trumpet, Gabriel. "Get to work, girl! No blue Monday 'round here." Ooo, better have no tracks when Aunt Duke come home, huh uh! Hurry, cook dinner now. Mmm, gumbo...my my! Quick, wash up...sun going down! Get those pots to shine. *(The lights fade.)* It's dark now...by the Mississippi. A big bunch of us all sitting 'round the campfire roasting acorns watching the boats moving down the river. Eating sugar cane, singing, having us a glorious time. Flames reaching up higher and higher and higher... I see you! *(pointing downstage left)* I know who you is. *(rises)* Demon! Leave me be! You can't stand against the blood of Jesus. *(frightened)* Death is here! He's a big raw-boney man with blazin' eyes. Death, you have no dominion over me! Step aside! You have to wait on King Jesus. *(calling right)* Jesus! You told me You'd be here. Jesus...*Jesus*! Oh, there You are. I was scared. I was calling for You. You remembered, didn't You? *(All fear is gone now as she starts toward Jesus. She* *stops.)* Lord, it's so dark here. *(The lights change.)* Oh, You throwed a handful of stars in our pathway. So bright, so bright! I see a river, Lord. *(She moves toward the river downstage right)* So still and lovely, trees on the other side. Nothing but beautiful evergreens. *(She stops.)* Lord, is this the River Jordan I got to cross?

*(She hears the Lord's answer, then sings **Take my Hand, Precious Lord**.)*

MAHALIA. PRECIOUS LORD, TAKE MY HAND,
LEAD ME ON, LET ME STAND.
I AM TIRED, I AM WEAK, I AM WORN.
THROUGH THE STORM, THROUGH THE NIGHT,
LEAD ME ON TO THE LIGHT.
TAKE MY HAND, PRECIOUS LORD, LEAD ME HOME.
WHEN MY WAY GROWS DREAR',
PRECIOUS LORD, LINGER NEAR,
WHEN MY LIFE IS ALMOST GONE,
AT THE RIVER I STAND,
GUIDE MY FEET, HOLD MY HAND,
TAKE MY HAND, PRECIOUS LORD, LEAD ME HOME.

*(The Lord takes **MAHALIA**'s hand and leads her across the Jordan as the lights fade.)*

WOMAN REPORTER. *(at stage right limbo she reads from The Chicago Tribune.)* Mahalia Jackson, a grandchild of plantation slaves whose full-throated voice carried her from birth in a three-room shanty to appearances before presidents and royalty, died January 27, 1972, at the age of 60 after a recent European tour. A spokesman at the Little Company of Mary Hospital in Chicago said the cause of death was heart failure. She left no immediate survivors. On Monday, January 31, more than 40,000 mourners filed past Mahalia Jackson's open coffin in Chicago's Greater Salem Baptist Church. Tuesday, 6,000 people jammed the Arie Crown Theatre at McCormick Place to attend funeral services. Her body was flown to New Orleans later that day.

MAN REPORTER. *(At stage left limbo he reads from The New Orleans Times Picayune.)* 60,000 citizens of New Orleans stood in line for hours outside the Rivergate Auditorium on Friday, waiting to pay final tribute to one of their own. Mahalia Jackson was buried today after a funeral that was attended by over 8,000 mourners. As marching bands played funeral dirges, mourners were led by the Governor of Louisiana and the Mayor of New Orleans to the gravesite at Providence Memorial Park where there was a brief ceremony. Afterward, the "second line" was formed and the bands burst forth in a medley of gospel music as the procession began the return trip to the city; swinging and high stepping to the joyful sound.

WOMAN REPORTER. And the angels began to move over and make room for Mahalia, as she joined the heavenly choir.

(The limbo areas fade and a spot shines down on **MAHALIA** *upstage center. She is wearing golden shoes, a diadem, and a white robe that is trimmed with gold. She sings* **Move on up a Little Higher***.)*

ONE OF THESE MORNINGS, SOON ONE MORNING,
I'M GOIN' TO LAY DOWN MY CROSS AND GET MY CROWN.
SOON ONE EVENING, LATE IN THE EVENING, SOON ONE
    EVENING,
I'M GOING HOME TO LIVE ON HIGH.
WELL, AS SOON AS MY FEET STRIKE ZION,

(She steps off platform and all lights come up full as she crosses downstage center.)

I'M GOING TO LAY DOWN MY HEAVY BURDEN.
PUT ON MY ROBE IN GLORY, GOING TO SHOUT AND TELL
    MY STORY.
HOW I COME OVER HILLS AND MOUNTAINS.
I'M GOIN' TO DRINK FROM THE CRYSTAL FOUNTAINS.
YOU KNOW, ALL GOD'S SONS AND DAUGHTERS, THAT
    MORNIN',
WILL BE DRINKIN' THAT OLD HEALIN' WATER.

AND I'M GOIN' TO LIVE ON FOREVER,
I'M GOIN' TO LIVE ON FOREVER,
I'M GOIN' LIVE ON FOREVER AFTER A WHILE.

OH LORD, I'M GOIN' OUT SIGHTSEEING IN BEULAH.
MARCH ALL 'ROUND GOD'S ALTAR.
GOIN' TO WALK AND NEVER GET TIRED.
GOIN' TO TRY AND NEVER FALTER.

GONNA MOVE ON UP A LITTLE HIGHER, GONNA MEET MY
    LOVIN' MOTHER.
I'M GONNA MOVE ON UP A LITTLE HIGHER,
GONNA MEET THE LILY OF THE VALLEY.
I'M GONNA FEAST WITH THE ROSE OF SHARON.
IT WILL ALWAYS BE HOWDY, HOWDY.
IT WILL ALWAYS BE HOWDY, HOWDY.
IT WILL ALWAYS BE HOWDY, HOWDY AND NEVER GOODBYE.

(All the lights fade, except the "magic circle." **MAHALIA**
bows and the "magic circle" fades as the curtain falls.)

End of Play

WORKING PROPERTY LIST

ACT I PRESET
ONSTAGE:

Organ/bench–Left (start organ), Leslie speaker, telephone and Bible on small table by organ, New Orleans suitcase w/sweater Stage Left of organ, Piano/bench–Right, money on piano, baptismal gown/ stole on piano, bench Downstage Left, 3 bentwood chairs Upstage Center, 1 bentwood chair–Downstage Right

STAGE LEFT:

3 newspaper reviews, podium, 3 rolls and 2 stacks (15 ea.) of money, Francis' dark glasses, 2 concert collars, Dorsey coat and hat (20 bills in hat), Chicago preacher robe w/collar, 3 hairpins, Carnegie earrings, "angel" robe, diadem, gold shoes, Aunt Duke's apron.

STAGE RIGHT:

2 Montgomery suitcases, purse (w/brownie camera, pills, moccasins and TV remote), 3 wads and 2 stacks (15 ea.) of money, Stearns invitation, William Morris letter w/contract, glass of water, Carnegie suitcase (containing Carnegie gown, black high-heel shoes, and money), down-home preacher robe with cap, Mildred's blue suit w/ shoes, non-prop drinking water, Aunt Duke's flower hat, shawl, and hymnal.

DRESSING ROOM:

Money (Remind actors to load up.)

ACT II RESET
SET:

Podium to Stage Left limbo spike marks, Bible to Stage Right prop table, reset money, scarf for "Elijah Rock" on Downstage Left bench, Chicago Times for woman reporter on piano, New Orleans Times Picayune for man reporter on organ, Francis' blue hat Upstage end of organ, Francis' dark glasses to Stage Left prop table, wireless microphone at "on" position to piano, Francis' blue coat and clip-on bow tie to Stage Left wings. All actors need money.

STRIKE:

New Orleans suitcase with sweater, Carnegie suitcase (Hang up Carnegie gown.) various clothes.

COSTUME PLOT FOR ACT ONE

MAHALIA: Green dress (money must be able to go down the front), black low shoes, apron that covers as much as possible (scenes in New Orleans), white baptismal gown or stole (must be easy to "drape" on shoulders), light colored sweater (worn over shoulders on the train), black velvet Carnegie gown with white trim and train (the gown is not quite a robe that must go over Mahalia's green dress, zip up the front, and have a neckline that allows money to go down the front), black high heel shoes, rhinestone earrings, pony tail hair piece (pinned into a bun for Carnegie).

COUSIN FRED: Black pants, belt, white dress shirt, argyle sweater vest, black shoes, and black sox. (Actor wears same suit pants, belt, shirt, shoes, and sox for all characters.)

PASTOR LAWRENCE: Black preacher's robe with close fitting black preacher's cap.

CHICAGO PREACHER: Black Doctor of Divinity robe with academic hood.

DORSEY: Black suit with three-button jacket, red overhand tie, gray checkered vest, overcoat, and gray fedora.

FRANCIS: Black 3 pc. suit, white shirt, black clip-on bow tie, dark glasses. (White choir collar is added for Carnegie performance.)

AUNT DUKE: 1930's flowered dress, blue hat, purse, white gloves, overcoat, apron, with black shoes. Sunday hat and shawl for baptism scene.

MILDRED: 1940's brown suit, hat with feathers, overcoat, brown heels, under dressed with 1950's black dress (Carnegie), black heels and white choir collar (Carnegie).

ACCOMPANIST: 1930's woman's blue suit, cream blouse, and black heels ("Joshua Fit the Battle"). Carnegie dress w/out choir collar ("I'm Going to Live the Life").

COSTUME PLOT FOR ACT TWO

MAHALIA: Nondescript tan suit, cream colored blouse (money must go down the front), brown heels, large brown purse, Indian moccasins, long glamorous looking piece of lightweight material that can be draped as a shawl or stole ("Elijah Rock"), hair bun.

MILDRED: Nondescript maroon suit, light colored blouse, black heels.

KING: Black 3pc. suit, white shirt, narrow tie, tie clip, white pocket hankie.

FRANCIS: Cardigan sweater (rehearsal scene), lt. blue seersucker jacket, clip-on bow tie (church scene and remainder of play), add lt. blue snap-brim hat for Europe and Holy Land.

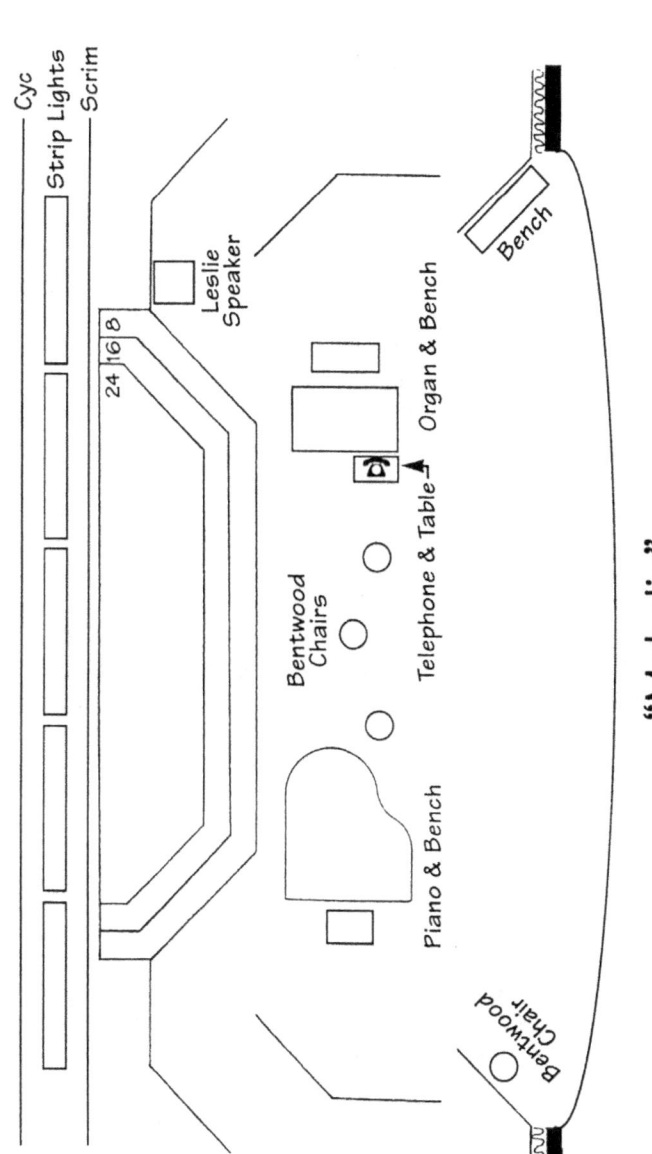

Cyc

Strip Lights

Scrim

24 16 8

Leslie Speaker

Organ & Bench

Telephone & Table

Bentwood Chairs

Piano & Bench

Bench

Bentwood Chair

"Mahalia"

OTHER TITLES AVAILABLE FROM SAMUEL FRENCH

THE WHIPPING MAN

Matthew Lopez

Drama / 3m

It is April, 1865. The Civil War is over and throughout the south, slaves are being freed, soldiers are returning home and in Jewish homes, the annual celebration of Passover is being celebrated. Into the chaos of war-torn Richmond comes Caleb DeLeon, a young Confederate officer who has been severely wounded. He finds his family's home in ruins and abandoned, save for two former slaves, Simon and John, who wait in the empty house for the family's return. As the three men wait for signs of life to return to the city, they wrestle with their shared past, the bitter irony of Jewish slave-owning and the reality of the new world in which they find themselves. The sun sets on the last night of Passover and Simon - having adopted the religion of his masters - prepares a humble Seder to observe the ancient celebration of the freeing of the Hebrew slaves from Egypt, noting with particular satisfaction the parallels to their current situation. But the pain of their enslavement will not be soothed by this tradition, and deep buried secrets from the past refuse to be hidden forever as the play comes to its shocking climax.

"A cause for celebration. Mathew Lopez has come as close as any author could to producing a microcosm of the genesis of a wide range of today's Black American males."
– Bob Rendell, *Talkin' Broadway*

"I can see why director Lou Bellamy chose this play for Penumbra, whose most famous alumnus is playwright August Wilson. In its complex welter of issues, in its interior explorations…*The Whipping Man* is Wilsonian."
– Rohan Preston, *Minneapolis Star-Ledger*

OTHER TITLES AVAILABLE FROM SAMUEL FRENCH

MOTHERHOUSE

Victor Lodato

Drama / 2m, 2f (Conceived for African-American actors, but casts of other races are possible) / Multiple sets

The play follows an African-American family in a low-income neighborhood whose lives are ultimately ruined by their surroundings. Clive arrives unexpectedly at the house of his mother and his sister. He says that he is fleeing from the police - but perhaps it's another one of his delusions. Unbeknownst to him, he has shown up on a tragic anniversary. Three years prior, his sister's child was killed in a brutal shooting. As fate seems bent on shattering the walls, mother Mae valiantly attempts to keep house.

Mr. Lodato is a 2002-2003 Guggenheim Fellow, as well as the recipient of the 2002 L. Arnold Weissberger Award for *Motherhouse*

OTHER TITLES AVAILABLE FROM SAMUEL FRENCH

GEE'S BEND

Elyzabeth Gregory Wilder

Drama / 1m, 3f / Simple Set

**2008 Harold and Mimi Steinberg/ATCA New Play Award —
American Theater Critics Association**

Gee's Bend depicts the turbulent history of African-Americans in the 20th century by focusing on a single family in the real community of Gee's Bend, Alabama, which is now famous for the beautiful quilts created by the women that grew up there. Gospel songs weave in and out of this hauntingly beautiful work.

"*Gee's Bend* is a lovefest – between the characters in the play and the land they live on, between the actors and the characters they're portraying, between the play and the audience."
– *Orlando Sentinel*

"Touching, lovely, and true."
– *Chicago Sun-Times*

OTHER TITLES AVAILABLE FROM SAMUEL FRENCH

BULRUSHER

Eisa Davis

Drama / 3m, 3f

In 1955, in the redwood country north of San Francisco, a multiracial girl grows up in a predominantly white town whose residents pepper their speech with the historical dialect of Boontling. Found floating in a basket on the river as an infant, Bulrusher is an orphan with a gift for clairvoyance that makes her feel like a stranger even amongst the strange: the taciturn schoolteacher who adopted her, the madam who runs her brothel with a fierce discipline, the logger with a zest for horses and women, and the guitar-slinging boy who is after Bulrusher's heart. Just when she thought her world might close in on her, she discovers an entirely new sense of self when a black girl from Alabama comes to town. Passionate, lyrical, and chock full of down-home humor, this play is an unforgettable experience by a new, thrilling voice.

Finalist for the 2007 Pulitzer Prize in Drama

"[Davis] tickles the ears of her listeners…moving scenes on the banks of the pebble-strewn river…feel utterly true."
– *The New York Times*

"Davis explores her themes in unexpected and evocative ways…The still waters of *Bulrusher* turn out to run pretty deep."
– *The San Francisco Chronicle*

"An engrossing rush…Eisa Davis' gleaming marriage of poetry and myth…has a big heart and a wide-open soul."
– *Minneapolis-St. Paul Star Tribune*

"*Bulrusher* brims with profound lyrical passion…a poetic play with much nuance…"
– *NYTheatre.com*

SAMUELFRENCH.COM